# HOLLY POINTE & CANDY CANES

CINDY KIRK

This is a work of fiction. Names, characters, places and incidents are products of the author's imagination or are used fictitiously. Any resemblance to actual events, locales, organizations, or persons, living or dead, is entirely coincidental.

ISBN: 978-1-7329601-9-0

# CHAPTER ONE

Faith Pierson had never played a contact sport. Which meant she'd never learned how to take a hit. That's why the body ramming into her at full speed had her stumbling.

She'd strolled into the Busy Bean Coffee & Tea Shop in downtown Holly Pointe, intent on grabbing a coffee and something sweet. The plan vanished as Faith swayed and fought to catch her breath.

"I'm so sorry." A firm grip settled on her arm, steadying her. "Are you okay?"

Faith looked up and found herself drowning in concerned hazel eyes.

"Wh-who are you?" Still reeling, she stammered the question.

"The father of the future linebacker who ran into you." The man cast a censuring look at the blonde girl with innocent blue eyes who stood before Faith.

Suddenly, where there had been one, there were now two. Faith blinked, but the mirror image remained.

She raised a hand to her head. Had the hit knocked something loose in her head?

"Please don't faint." The man spoke quickly and tightened his hold.

Faith blinked. She blinked again. When she spoke, her voice was reed-thin with barely contained panic. "I-I'm seeing double."

He offered a reassuring smile. "You're fine."

"I'm not," she insisted. "You don't understand. There's *two*."

"Twins." He kept hold of her with one hand and pointed with the other. "Charlotte and Hannah. Charlotte is the one who tackled you."

His gaze settled on the girl with a hint of mischief in her eyes. "What do you say to the lady, Charlotte?"

"I'm sorry." A dimple winked briefly at the corner of her mouth. "Me and Hannah were playing tag. I couldn't let her catch me."

"I've already told you this is a coffee shop, not a playground." The man's stern expression shifted from one girl to the other. "You both know better."

Hannah hopped from one foot to the other, appearing to take the rebuke in stride.

Charlotte didn't hop, but her blue eyes studied Faith with a thoroughness that had her wondering if there was something on her face.

She was ready to pull out a mirror when the child spoke. "You have dancing reindeers on your shirt."

"I like reindeers. Especially ones wearing ballet shoes." Hannah stepped closer and pointed at Faith's chest. "Does that bell ring?"

This morning, Faith had pulled on her favorite December outfit—a red plaid corduroy jumper with a turtleneck covered in dancing reindeer. A necklace with a large jingle bell completed the festive look.

Lifting the red braided cord, Faith held out the bell so it emitted a faint clang. "Want to give it a jingle?"

Hannah nodded even as Charlotte wedged herself between Faith and her twin.

"The lady asked me first." Hannah tried with both hands to push Charlotte to the side, but failed. "Daaad, make her move."

Faith wrapped her fingers around the bell. She loved children, no matter how young or old. This age—she'd guess the girls to be five or six—was a particular favorite. "Christmas is about love and goodwill. Right?"

The girls stopped shoving each other and exchanged a glance. Then they both nodded.

Relieved, Faith grinned, conscious that their father's scrutinizing gaze remained on her.

"You both want to ring the bell." Faith tapped a finger against her bright-red lips. "I believe I have a solution."

Lifting the necklace over her head, Faith shortened the cord before placing it around Hannah's neck. "Don't ring it just yet. Understand?"

With a wide-eyed gaze fixed on Faith, Hannah nodded. Her small hand curved around the bell the way Faith's fingers had only moments before.

Tears of frustration filled Charlotte's eyes, and her bottom lip quivered.

Diving deep into the cavernous depths of her quilted purse, Faith quickly pulled out another necklace, identical to the one she'd given Hannah.

When Faith slipped this one over Charlotte's neck, she was rewarded with a big smile that showed two missing teeth.

"Now we're ready." Faith lifted a hand. "On the count of three, you'll jingle."

"I don't think—" Their father shot a swift glance around the shop. "The noise will disturb the other customers."

"No worries." Faith flashed a reassuring smile. "This is Holly Pointe. We love all things Christmas. That includes jingling sleigh bells."

Returning her attention to the girls, Faith counted off. "One. Two. Three."

When the third finger went up, the girls rang the bells loudly.

The jingling caught the attention of those in the shop. Instead of grumbles, the sound prompted only indulgent smiles. Behind the counter, shop owners Kenny and Norma Douglas applauded.

"Thank you for the lovely concert, girls." Faith turned to their father. Now that she was steady again, she realized she'd forgotten her manners. She extended her hand. "I'm Faith Pierson."

The smile he offered as his hand closed over hers held warmth and apology. "Graham Westfall. It's a pleasure to meet you. I'm sorry it was under these circumstances."

Graham was a handsome man about her own age, with dark hair cut short and a firm jaw. Despite it being barely nine in the morning, lines of strain edged his eyes.

Faith had initially thought his eyes were hazel. Studying him now, she saw a shimmer of green with gold flecks. Attraction stirred. She'd always been a sucker for green eyes.

She wondered what had brought him to Holly Pointe. If he was visiting relatives, wouldn't they be with him? Of course, he could have come for the skiing. Jay Peak was just down the road. Many tourists, especially those with children, often chose to stay in Holly Pointe, even while on a ski vacation, because of the community's family-centered activities.

As those amazing green eyes had her wanting to flirt—though flirting wasn't her strength—Faith reminded herself that just because he wasn't wearing a wedding ring, didn't mean there wasn't a wife, perhaps in the restroom or even back at a hotel. "Are you visiting family in the area, Mr. Westfall?"

"I think being tackled by my daughter puts us on a first-name basis." His eyes crinkled at the corners. "Please, call me Graham."

She returned his smile. There was that tingle again. One she ruthlessly tamped down.

*Possible wife in the restroom,* she reminded herself.

Still, she couldn't stop herself from offering a teasing smile. "Only if you call me Faith."

"Well, Faith, in answer to your question, the girls and I arrived today." Graham shot a quick glance at a nearby table filled with coloring books and what appeared to be a jewelry-making kit. "My mother-in-law, Ginny Blain, lives in Holly Pointe."

*Mother-in-law.*

Suddenly, it struck Faith, a swift hammer blow to the heart. Ginny had had only one daughter, *Stephanie.*

This was Stephanie's husband. Though Faith hadn't grown up in Holly Pointe, she'd met Steph as a young girl. Steph had been pretty and vivacious, with an energy that drew you to her. As Ginny was Faith's grandmother's best friend, Faith knew all about the tragic accident that had claimed her life.

"I'm so sorry." The words tumbled out before she could stop them.

Surprise had his eyes widening for just a second. Then his expression became unreadable. He didn't ask why she was sorry. "Thank you. It's been a difficult three years."

Faith had been in Holly Pointe only a few months when Ginny had received a call that her only daughter had been badly injured in a car accident. At the time, the young woman had been living in Manhattan with her husband and twin toddlers. Before Ginny could get to New York, Steph passed away. The twins had survived the crash without a scratch.

"Won't you please join us? Give us a chance to make up for the trouble we caused."

Faith hesitated. She'd planned on this trip to the Busy Bean being a quick in-and-out. The holidays were a busy time at Faith Originals.

Still, Ginny was her grandmother's best friend. Graham was a visitor in her town. Making him feel welcome was the least she could do.

She needed only one thing first. *Caffeine.*

"Thank you. I'd love to get better acquainted. First, let me grab a cup of coffee."

"Tell me what you want, and I'll get it. My treat." He lifted a staying hand when she opened her mouth to protest. "Please. I owe you. My daughter upended you like a nose guard going for the quarterback."

"That's a bit of an exaggeration, don't you think?" The child might have made contact, but if Faith had been paying attention, she could have evaded her. By now, she'd be at the goalposts, er, counter, with a large coffee in hand.

Faith wished Graham would drop the idea of paying, but the determined gleam in those gorgeous green eyes told her that wasn't happening. "Just so we're clear—you don't owe me anything. However, since you insist, I'd love a cup of the Snickerdoodle-flavored coffee."

Graham cocked his head. "Cream? Sugar?"

"Black."

His grin flashed. "One coffee coming right up."

Faith felt the tingle again. Heck, maybe the impact with Charlotte *had* knocked something loose.

Two pairs of curious eyes settled on Faith as she took a seat at the cluttered table.

"Hi, girls. I'm Faith." With a sweep of one hand, Faith gestured to the tabletop. "Looks like you've got a lot to keep you busy."

A partially finished bracelet made of beads sat in front of Charlotte. A coloring book lay open in front of Hannah.

The pleasant rumble of Kenny's laughter had Faith shifting her focus to where Graham was conversing with the shop's owners.

"We're bored."

Faith pulled her attention from the counter and back to the twins. "Really?"

Hannah nodded. Her gaze lingered on a window decorated with snowflake decals. "I want to build a snowman."

Charlotte's mouth formed a pout. "I want to go sledding."

"I'm betting you'll be outside real soon." Though it was cozy-warm inside the Busy Bean, Faith couldn't imagine Graham intended to keep the girls inside all day.

"We were supposed to be at Gramma's house," Charlotte told her. "Uncle Shawn was there, so we had to leave."

Hannah nodded in agreement.

Faith decided the child must have misunderstood. Ginny would never turn away Graham. Or her grandchildren.

Graham returned with not only a cup of steaming coffee, but a freshly baked scone, complete with clotted cream and strawberry jam. "Norma thought you might like this. She said something about it being fresh out of the oven."

Faith caught Norma's eye and mouthed, "Thank you."

Charlotte zeroed in on the pastry like a heat-seeking missile. "Can I have some of it?"

Hannah's hand shot up as if in a classroom. "Me, too. Please."

"Please," Charlotte hurriedly added.

"There's enough here for everyone." Faith picked up a knife and waggled it at Graham. "That includes your dad."

Ignoring his protest, Faith cut the scone in fourths and gestured to the twins.

The girls needed no encouragement to grab a slice.

When she held out the plate to Graham, he shook his head. "The scone was for you. Now it's half gone."

"More than enough." Faith gestured with the knife. "Two pieces. One for me. One for you."

Graham appeared to be doing his best to suppress a smile as he chose the smallest piece. "Are you always this bossy?"

"Sometimes I'm worse."

"Good to know." He chuckled. "And thank you."

"You're welcome." Faith added a dab of clotted cream to the top of her piece, while the girls claimed the jam.

Moments later, Graham sat back and expelled a satisfied breath. "I have to say that was as good as anything I've had in the city."

Faith popped the last bit of scone into her mouth and let the taste roll around on her tongue. She considered the bakeries she'd frequented when she lived—and worked—in Manhattan. He was right.

"Truer words." She inclined her head. "Do you still live in Manhattan?"

Surprise flickered in his eyes as he took a long drink of coffee. Surely he didn't believe Ginny never spoke of him or the girls.

"Upper West Side. Across from the park." His gaze shifted once again to his daughters. "I'm amazed they have room in their stomachs after the breakfast they consumed."

Faith was glad to hear the girls had eaten something more substantial than a bite of scone for breakfast. "I'm not surprised. Ginny is an excellent cook."

"Actually, once we got into town, our first stop was Rosie's Diner." Graham's tone remained easy as his gaze slid to the twins, who were busy eating leftover jam with a spoon. "It seemed rude to arrive on Ginny's doorstep with two hungry girls expecting to be fed."

"I bet she was super excited to see you." Regardless of Charlotte's words, Faith knew Ginny wouldn't turn away family.

"Things were a bit hectic. Steph's brother, Shawn, and his family unexpectedly showed up last night. No notice, but none was needed. Ginny has an open-door policy when it comes to her kids."

Shawn and his wife, Morgan, had married right out of high school and now had three teenage boys. Though Ginny didn't gossip about her kids, Faith knew Shawn and Morgan lived in New Hampshire and struggled to make ends meet.

"Ginny made it clear they'd make room for us." Graham cradled the cup between his hands, and the lines around his eyes deepened. "Shawn was all for it. He's one of those 'the more, the merrier' kind of guys. Me, I gave up sleeping on sofas back in college."

"Air mattresses, Daddy, not the sofa." Charlotte look up from her coloring. "I think sleeping in Gramma's living room sounds like fun."

"If this wasn't a working vacation for me," Graham told Faith, "I might have tried to make it work. But I wouldn't be able to concentrate with the kids and the dog and—"

"Ginny doesn't have a dog," Faith interrupted.

"Shawn and his wife have a bearded collie," Graham informed her. "They brought him along."

Faith pulled her brows together. "I'm not sure I've ever seen that kind of collie."

"Think massive sheepdog. One that knocks over anything—and anyone—in its way."

Not even trying to suppress a smile, Faith grinned. "I take it you're not an animal lover."

"I like them fine, just not in a twelve-hundred-square-foot house that's already housing three adults and three adult-sized boys."

"Good point." Faith understood now why he and the girls weren't staying with Ginny. "Are any of Ginny's other kids coming home for Christmas?"

"From what Ginny said, Seth is spending the holidays with his wife's side of the family." Graham rubbed his chin. "Spence is still in Dubai. He won't come back for a visit until next year."

"They have camels where Uncle Spencer lives," Hannah informed Faith. "One day, I'm going to go there and ride one."

"Me, too," Charlotte told her sister before turning to Faith. "It's like riding a pony, only bumpier."

Faith smiled. "My brother and his friend once raced camels."

The girls' eyes turned as big as saucers before suspicion clouded Charlotte's baby blues. "Are you making that up?"

Graham's equally skeptical look had Faith chuckling.

"My brother once lived in Dubai. He and his friend worked for General Mills, their Middle East and Africa division, for a time." Seeing that the information had done nothing to convince the twins, Faith added, "I've got pictures."

"Do you remember when your uncle sent you pictures of him riding the camel?" Graham asked his daughters.

"Maybe my uncle knows your brother." Charlotte sat upright, and her eyes brightened. "What if they rode camels together?"

"Stranger things have happened." Though Faith knew in a city of three million, it was unlikely Evan and Spencer had met.

Charlotte picked up a crayon, leaving Faith able to focus on Graham. "When did Spencer move to Dubai? Last I knew, he was in San Francisco."

"He accepted a job there last May." He took a long drink of coffee. "Spence heads the marketing and communications division of a firm that deals in freight management and contract logistics on a global level."

"I'm not even sure what that means." Faith offered a little laugh. "It sounds impressive."

"Spence is a go-getter, that's for sure." Graham inclined his head. "What about you?"

Instead of telling him about her shop, Faith tapped a finger against her lips. "I'd say I'm more of a slow-getter than a go-getter."

*An endless disappointment to my parents*, she thought with a sigh.

The girls giggled.

"You're a slow-getter." Charlotte pointed to her sister.

"Nuh-uh." Hannah shook her head. "I'm a go-getter. You're the slow-getter."

"Girls." Graham's tone held a sharp edge, and the teasing instantly ceased.

When Graham refocused on Faith, he studied her with curious eyes. She braced herself for more questions about her "career," which would undoubtedly be followed by "encouraging words." While usually meant to be supportive, such encouragement always made her feel like she should be doing more.

*Wasted potential.* That's what her father had declared.

Faith lifted her chin. She didn't care what anyone thought. She loved her business and the life she was building in Holly Pointe.

She didn't have to justify the choices she'd made. Not to her parents. Not to this stranger. Not to anyone.

Graham shrugged. "The girls and I were disappointed with the change in plans."

For a second, Faith was confused. Then she realized he'd moved on in the conversation. He didn't intend to interrogate her or make judgments. Likely because how she lived her life was of little concern to him.

"I gave our nanny the month off for her sister's wedding." Graham's fingers curved around the ceramic coffee cup. "I have a project that absolutely must be completed by the end of December. I figured Ginny would get her twin-time. I could put in the hours on the project undisturbed. Win-win for all."

He shot another glance at the twins, who were now intently licking out the little silver cups that had once held jam and cream. Shaking his head, he continued. "We flew into Burlington this morning, then rented a car and drove the rest of the way here."

"What will you do now?"

"I've been calling around. Every place I've checked is either booked or the accommodations don't meet my needs."

Curious, Faith lifted her cup. "Which are?"

"A suite, rather than simply a hotel room." He glanced at the girls, now busily coloring, then back at Faith. "I need space to work. The girls need space to play."

Faith nodded.

"We may end up returning to the city. That would be unfortunate. I know Ginny was looking forward to spending this time with the girls. But—" Graham expelled a breath and shrugged. "Well, we'll see."

Faith thought of the second floor of her grandmother's home, an area that sat empty between Thanksgiving and New Year's.

The space would be perfect for Graham and the girls.

"There's a suite of rooms on the second floor of my grandmother's house that's available." Faith's tone turned persuasive. "There's a small kitchen and sitting area, as well as two bedrooms, each with their own bath. Trust me when I say you won't find anything nicer in the area."

Suspicion clouded Graham's assessing gaze. "If the space is so nice, why isn't it already rented?"

It was a valid question and one she'd have asked in his position. "My grandmother doesn't normally rent it out in December. With the main floor of the house turning into a Christmas wonderland, the downstairs becomes a noisy beehive. Your girls will likely love all the activity, but if you like to work in the quiet, I suggest noise-canceling headphones."

Interest flickered in his green depths. "How much?"

The rates normally went up during ski season, but because Graham was with Ginny's granddaughters, Faith gave him the summer monthly rate.

She wanted him to take it. For Ginny's sake, she wanted him to stay.

Faith offered him a bright smile. "Interested in a tour?"

# CHAPTER TWO

Following Faith's direction, Graham pulled into the driveway that ran alongside the massive Victorian house. Despite the falling snow, she waited for him and the twins on the porch.

Though Graham preferred modern structures, he had to admit the home, with its towers, turrets and wraparound porch, caught his eye. For a house that had been built more than a hundred years ago, it was remarkably well maintained. A coat of fresh paint covered the cedar siding, and the roof appeared new.

"You could have waited inside," Graham told her as he climbed the steps and a gust of wind slapped his face. "Aren't you cold?"

"Not at all." The good-natured chuckle seemed as much a part of her as her puffy red coat and striped stocking cap. She gestured to the snow-covered lawn. "Volunteers are coming this afternoon to finish decorating the exterior. The Candy Cane Christmas House is a community endeavor."

"Candy Cane Christmas House?" Charlotte perked up. "Will there be lots of candy?"

Hannah raised her hand. "I'd like a candy cane, please."

"You've both had enough sweets for now." Graham kept his

tone matter-of-fact even as his heart gave a ping. Steph had loved candy canes.

Faith pushed the door open and called out, "It's just me. I brought guests."

"I'm in the kitchen," a distant voice responded.

After stepping into the foyer, Charlotte paused to study a nutcracker that topped her by a foot. Hannah appeared more interested in the garland wound around the banister.

Graham had to admit the greenery was eye-catching with its red ribbons and red-and-white candy ornaments.

The candy and peppermint theme continued down the hall. When they entered the second parlor, his gaze was drawn to a large evergreen in the corner.

"Oh." Hannah's eyes went wide. "It's be-u-ti-ful."

Faith smiled, obviously pleased by Hannah's reaction.

Graham wasn't surprised his daughter was impressed. The tree had everything a child loved—rotating ornaments, twinkle lights and lots of glitter.

"We call it our Candy Land Christmas Tree," Faith explained with an indulgent smile. "What do you think of the elf ladders? They're new this year."

Two small ladders nestled into the branches on each side of the tree. Stuffed elves were posed on the steps as if in the middle of decorating the tree.

Graham struggled for a polite, yet suitable response.

"That one is my favorite." Charlotte made a beeline for one of the elves.

"You brought guests."

The unexpected voice had Charlotte stopping in her tracks and whirling.

An older woman with white hair and skin so pale it appeared translucent stepped into the room, a silver tray wobbling in her hands.

"Let me help you with that." Graham hurried to take the tray from her. "Where would you like me to set this?"

"On the credenza would be lovely." Brushing a strand of hair back from her face, the woman lowered herself into the closest chair as if she couldn't stand for a moment longer.

"You've been baking."

Instead of concern, Graham heard pleasure and approval in Faith's voice.

"I can't claim credit." The older woman chuckled. "Stella and Melinda stopped over. They insisted on baking cookies for this afternoon's volunteers."

"That was nice of them." Faith's voice might be easy, but the light in her eyes had dimmed. "Did you help?"

"I supervised."

"Ahh." Faith gestured to the woman. "Girls, Graham. This is my grandmother, Mary Pierson."

Graham studied Mary. The shape of her eyes reminded him of Faith's. "It's a pleasure to meet you."

"Grandmother, this is Graham Westfall and his daughters, Charlotte," Faith pointed to the one girl then to the other, "and Hannah. These two cuties are Ginny's granddaughters."

"Ginny has talked of little else but your arrival. It's kind of you to bring the girls over to meet me." Mary gestured to the credenza. "I realize it's nearly time for lunch, but would you like a cookie?"

Charlotte and Hannah cast imploring looks in Graham's direction.

*Christmas*, he reminded himself. "I'm sure the girls would love a cookie."

Graham realized when they each took two that he should have specified only one.

"Can we look at the train?" Hannah pointed with a cookie toward the track at the far end of the parlor.

A Christmas-themed train chugged around a festive holiday

village. Graham understood why it captured his daughters' interest. There were decorated trees, elves and even Rudolph the Red-Nosed Reindeer.

"Puh-leeze, Daddy." Charlotte put a hand to her throat in a dramatic gesture.

"Look, but don't touch. And what do you say to Mrs. Pierson?"

"Thank you for the cookies," the girls chimed in unison.

Mary's lips curved. "You're very welcome."

Faith's gaze followed the children across the room.

"They're darling." Mary's smile grew wistful. "I remember when my children were that age. Christmas is a magical time for the young."

"The holiday magic can continue into adulthood…if we embrace the season." As Faith took a seat on the sofa and gestured for him to do the same, the edge to her voice took Graham by surprise.

"How long will you be in Holly Pointe, Graham? I know Ginny was hoping you'd stay through Christmas."

"The girls and I were planning to stay the entire month." Graham hesitated. "We've run into a bit of a scheduling snafu with lodging."

"Shawn and his family arrived last night," Faith told her grandmother. "They're staying with Ginny."

The look in Mary's eyes told Graham she understood. "Ginny's home isn't big enough to house two families."

"It isn't," Graham agreed.

"I offered Graham the use of the second floor while he's in town," Faith explained. "I warned that it'll be hectic on the main floor."

"What exactly goes on here?" he asked.

Before Faith could answer, the twins were back, bored with watching a train they couldn't touch.

"People come to bake cookies together, to make ornaments

and wrap gifts for underprivileged children and soldiers." Faith paused. "We have classes in candy-making and wreath-making. The gingerbread-house-making is especially popular. Santa comes here for pictures. There's—"

"Santa comes here?" Hannah asked, her eyes wide.

"To this house?" Charlotte clarified.

"He does indeed." The twinkle returned to Faith's eyes. "The Candy Cane Christmas House is one of the busiest places in Holly Pointe during December."

"That tree," Charlotte pointed to a bare evergreen in the far corner, "doesn't look very Christmasy."

Hannah expelled a heavy sigh. "Poor, sad tree."

"That is a memory tree." Faith gestured with one hand. "During the month, people will place something on the tree in memory of someone who has passed."

"I never decorated a tree before," Charlotte announced.

Surprise skittered across Faith's face. "You don't put up one at Christmas?"

"People bring the tree to our apartment and decorate it. They're experts," Hannah's expression turned earnest. "We're not allowed to touch."

"Or help," Charlotte added. "Sometimes Tiffany lets us watch them put it up."

"Tiffany?" Faith asked.

"Our nanny," Charlotte explained.

"We love her," Hannah added. "She's taken care of us since we were itty-bitty babies."

"Tiffany is a gem." Graham spoke in a hearty tone, then turned to the twins. "This year, we'll put up a tree, and you can help decorate it."

Hannah clapped. "Yay."

"Can we do it now?" Charlotte asked.

"First, we need a place to stay," Graham reminded her.

Faith turned to her grandmother. "Mary, would you mind watching the girls while I show Graham the upstairs?"

Mary smiled at the twins. "Perhaps you can help me load the dishwasher."

"We've never done that before." Charlotte glanced at her sister. "We don't know how."

Mary awkwardly rose to her feet. "There's always a first time."

Leaving the girls in the older woman's hands, Graham followed Faith up the stairs.

When they reached the top, she pulled out a key and unlocked a wooden door.

A thought struck him. "Do you live here, too?"

"I do." She inclined her head, her expression puzzled. "I thought I made that clear."

He shook his head. "You said this was your grandmother's house, but never mentioned you live here."

Graham realized that while Faith seemed to know much about him via Ginny, he knew little to nothing about her. "Are you married?"

The abrupt question, coming as it did out of left field, appeared to startle her as much as it did him.

She quickly rallied, shaking her head. "No husband. And, though you didn't ask, no children."

"How long have you lived in Holly Pointe?"

"Why all the questions?"

"It struck me that I've been doing all the talking."

She waved a dismissive hand. "We've been getting acquainted."

"Getting acquainted is when both people share." He offered an encouraging smile and repeated, "How long have you lived in Holly Pointe?"

She shut the upstairs door behind them before answering. "Three years ago, my grandmother came down with a bad case of pneumonia. It hit her hard. She tried to carry on as usual, but was weaker than she realized and fell. I quit my job and came to help her recuperate. I liked it here so much, I stayed."

"She's still unsteady."

"She's much better." Faith's gaze turned distant. "You should have seen her before, so energetic and full of life."

"Have you considered physical therapy? My uncle had hip surgery, and working with a therapist made all the difference."

Faith rested her back against the doorjamb. "Mary has seen lots of different therapists. She's physically capable of doing more. She just can't seem to motivate herself. And yes, before you suggest a counselor, I've tried, and she won't go."

"I'm sorry to hear of her troubles." Graham nearly reached out to squeeze her hand. He stopped himself just in time. "She's lucky to have someone like you in her corner."

"Thank you. I'm hoping this will be the Christmas she decides to embrace life again." She expelled a breath. "Let me show you around."

Graham glanced back at the parlor. "You said you rent this area out. Do you ever worry about giving strangers such easy access to your personal space?"

"We normally keep the door locked. There's an alternative entrance guests can use that takes them directly outside." Faith flicked on the lights in the sitting room. "If you decide to stay with us, you can come in through the front."

His gaze flickered over the furniture, then shifted to the flat-screen television mounted on one wall. With the exception of the TV, the room had a comfortable, vintage feel.

The tour took less than five minutes. "We updated the electrical two years ago and added more outlets."

"This is nice."

Faith lifted her hands, palms out. "I need to warn you that the internet can be unreliable. Most of the time, it isn't a problem, but when it is, it's a hassle."

Recalling how his GPS had gone wonky during the stormy drive to Holly Pointe, Graham understood.

"We'd love for you and the girls to stay with us. As long as you're sure the noise won't bother you."

Graham's lips quirked. "As long as the noise from the twins won't bother you."

"They won't be a problem." She returned his smile. "I assume they'll be spending a lot of time at Ginny's anyway."

"Well, despite the warnings, I'd love to take you up on your offer and stay."

Her smile returned, bright and hot.

Something inside him stirred.

"If you need anything, please let Mary or me know." Faith's phone buzzed, and she pulled it from a pocket. After glancing at the screen, she offered an apologetic smile. "I need to take this."

Graham watched her disappear down the stairs. Through the open door, the sounds of the twins' laughter drifted up. Though he knew he should head down and get the bags from the car, Graham dropped into a chair and exhaled a heavy breath.

He liked order in both his personal and business life, yet during the past few weeks, nothing had gone as planned.

The campaign he'd presented to one of the firm's top clients had bombed. He'd gone into that boardroom confident they were going to love his ideas.

When they'd only glanced at each other when he finished, a cold chill had engulfed his body. Apparently, he'd failed to capture the "feel" of their brand. His boss had given him thirty days to come up with a totally different campaign, one they loved, or he was off the project. And though it hadn't been said, his promotion to partner would be delayed. Which meant this had to be a working vacation.

That had suited him just fine, until he'd realized Tiffany would be gone the entire month. That was when he'd come up with an alternative plan. He'd take the twins to Vermont, and Ginny would keep them busy.

Now, due to Shawn's unexpected appearance, Graham was once again forced to regroup.

At least he'd found a decent place for them to stay. Graham surveyed his surroundings.

Faith had warned it could get noisy downstairs...

*Faith.* She was a refreshing change from the women he'd known since Steph's death.

Not that Faith Pierson fell into the category of someone he'd like to date. She wasn't his type.

Still, the woman exuded a refreshing calm that drew him in.

He chuckled. *Drew him in?* He must be more tired than he'd thought.

With the sounds of Faith's voice and his children's laughter wafting up the stairs, Graham trudged down to the car to get their luggage.

# CHAPTER THREE

Graham knew he should have texted Ginny immediately once he'd found a place to stay. But unpacking had taken more time than he'd anticipated. Then he'd needed groceries.

It was late afternoon when Ginny's car pulled in beside his rental at the Little Giant Market. When he saw she was alone, he seized the opportunity.

Shoving his hands into his coat pockets, Graham waited for her to get out of her car. When she did, he flashed a smile to let her know there were no hard feelings.

Her gently lined face, surrounded by dark hair generously peppered with silver, held worry. "Oh, Graham. I was planning to call you. I'm so sorry. I had no idea Shawn and Morgan planned to—"

Graham kept the smile on his lips. "No worries. I understand."

Gratitude filled the woman's blue eyes, eyes she'd passed down to her daughter and granddaughters.

"I'd let Shawn know that I'd bought his family Jay Peak lift tickets for Christmas. The plant where Shawn works closes for two weeks every December. I guess I should have expected..." Ginny paused. "They don't have the money to pay for lodging."

"Ginny." Graham gentled his tone. "It's okay. Honest."

"I never want you to feel like you and the girls aren't welcome anytime." Ginny met his gaze. "You are all my children."

From the moment he'd met her, Graham had found Ginny to be warm and welcoming. His mother-in-law had visited them regularly when their busy lives had kept him and Steph in the city.

"Rooms are nearly impossible to come by this time of year." Worry furrowed Ginny's brow. "Have you found anything?"

"I have." Graham took her arm and walked with her toward the store entrance. "The girls and I are staying at a private home right here in Holly Pointe."

Panic filled Ginny's eyes as it appeared to register for the first time that her granddaughters weren't with him. "Tell me you didn't leave the girls with strangers."

The accusation hit the mark. Leaving them with strangers was exactly what he'd done. When Faith had mentioned the girls could stay with her while he bought groceries, he'd hesitated. The twins had begged to stay. They'd wanted to help decorate the outside of the house. He'd bundled them up in their snowsuits and left them. With strangers. But were they, really?

"Mary and Faith Pierson." His gaze searched hers. "I understand they're friends of yours."

Relief blanketed her face as the automatic doors slid open, and they stepped into blessed warmth. "Is that who's watching the girls?"

Graham nodded. "They're putting up outside Christmas decorations this afternoon. Charlotte and Hannah wanted to help."

Her expression turned wistful. "I wish I could be there with them."

He offered an encouraging smile. "It's still going on. I know the twins would enjoy having you there."

"I wish I could, but I can't." She grabbed a shopping cart, but didn't move. The look in her eyes pleaded for understanding. "I promised Shawn's boys we'd make pizza this afternoon."

"Maybe we can all get together for pizza soon. The twins would enjoy getting to know their cousins." Graham wouldn't invite himself over, but he wanted to let her know he was open to the possibility.

"I'd love for them to get better acquainted." Ginny's flash of a smile gave him hope. "Once you get the girls settled and I get things organized at home, that's just what we'll do."

"Sounds like a good plan."

Ginny nodded. "I better get shopping for the food, or there'll be a mutiny. Don't you worry. I plan to spend lots of time with my granddaughters while you're here. We'll make Christmas special for the girls."

Graham left Ginny to her shopping and went to retrieve a cart of his own, her words circling in his head.

*Make Christmas special...*

When the twins had admitted they'd never decorated a tree, it had been a hard punch to the gut. They'd been so excited when he promised they'd put up a tree this year and they could decorate it.

Each Christmas, he'd showered the twins with gifts. But had he spent enough time with them? He'd done the best he could with a busy work schedule...

Even in his own head, it sounded like a cop-out.

Graham vowed this year would be different. He would work on the presentation—his job hung in the balance, after all—but he'd make spending time with the girls a priority.

This year would be a Christmas they'd all remember.

After an hour, Faith quit watching for Graham. She was too busy supervising the twins and the volunteers who'd arrived with one goal: turning the lawn into a candy cane wonderland.

"It's amazing," Faith told her friend Melinda Kelly, "how much you can get done when people work together."

Mel straightened a candy cane that, at six feet, was only a couple inches taller than her. With her fiery red hair, fair complexion and freckles, Mel was more striking than beautiful.

She was also smart and funny and one of Faith's best friends.

Like Faith, Mel had quit her job to return to Holly Pointe to help out a family member. In Mel's case, it was her mother. Rosie had pretty much run the family diner single-handedly until complications following knee surgery had sidelined her.

Although she'd fully recovered now, she was getting older and was happy to have her daughter at her side.

"I love these new canes." Mel patted the one she'd just erected. "They absorb light from the sun and glow in the dark. At night, they'll light a path—along with all the other canes—to the front steps."

"They are cool." Faith measured the distance between this one and the last. Though the lawn was full of people, there was a design plan, and everyone was following it.

"Thank goodness the snow quit." Mel craned her head back and studied the two men who were adding strings of lights to the eaves in a carefully ordered pattern.

"I'm glad they got the roof peak clips and the lights installed when there was no snow on the shingles." Faith narrowed her gaze. "I wish they'd gotten the lights up last week. I don't like them up that high."

"Derek and Zach are used to heights. They're builders and on roofs as much as they're on the ground." Mel glanced in the direction of the porch. "Where's Mary?"

There had been a time, one they both remembered, when Faith's grandmother would have been in the yard, chatting with volunteers and working twice as hard as everyone else.

"She's watching the twins." Faith chose her words carefully.

She felt disloyal saying anything that could possibly be construed as negative.

Good friend that she was, Mel let that go. She didn't mention that the twins had been out in the yard until a few minutes ago.

Mel put a hand on Faith's arm. "She just came out."

"What? Where?"

Faith jerked her attention just in time to see Mary set a tray of disposable cups on a card table that had been set up on the porch. One of the twins—from this distance, Faith couldn't tell which one—held the door open.

The twins hopped down the steps just as volunteers surged toward the porch for refreshments.

"Break time." Mel dusted the snow off her gloves. "Let's see what the drink of choice is this afternoon."

Faith's gloved hands had just curved around a cup of hot apple cider when she saw Graham coming around the side of the house.

When their eyes met, Faith felt her heart skip a beat.

Sipping her own cider, Mel lifted a brow. "Looks like Daddy's back."

"Yes." Faith returned his wave.

She thought—hoped—he'd stroll over so she could introduce him to Mel. Instead, Graham skirted the crowd to go to the twins. He scooped up a handful of snow and packed it on the large round ball that made up the base of what would eventually become a monster snowman.

"He was in the diner this morning." Mel's eyes sparkled. "I was cooking, so he didn't notice me. I noticed him."

Faith understood. There was something about the confident set to the man's shoulders and that ready smile. Not to mention, Graham was as handsome as all get-out.

"Look how he's lifting one of the twins up so she can place her snow on top of the mound." Her dad used to do that, Faith remembered, when her family came to Holly Pointe in the winter.

That was when all it had taken for her to make him proud was being a good sport and a hard worker. Once she got older, she hadn't been able to meet his expectations. Not if she wanted to fulfill her own dreams.

Her parents meant the world to her. Knowing she disappointed them every day by choosing to build a life in Holly Pointe was a bitter pill.

Mary understood. Had always understood.

Faith shifted her focus back to the porch and saw the cups of steaming cider on the tray her grandmother had brought out were nearly gone.

While Faith watched, Mary reached for the rail as if needing support.

"I'm going to check on my grandmother," Faith said to Mel. "I don't want her to overdo it."

Concern filled Mel's eyes. "Do you need help?"

"I should be fine." Faith glanced up to the roof. "I appreciate you and your brother taking time off work to come over and help."

"We're friends. Besides, decorating the Candy Cane Christmas House is one Holly Pointe tradition I don't want to see fall by the wayside." Mel's expression grew serious. "I swear, when Mary decided to skip the past couple of years, the entire community went into mourning."

"These past years have been hard on her." Faith had gone through withdrawal as well. Though there were a zillion and one other activities in Holly Pointe in December, Christmas hadn't been the same.

Giving Mel a hug, Faith covered the walkway in long strides and soon stood beside her grandmother on the porch. To her surprise, Mary appeared steady. Her cheeks held healthy color, and her eyes were bright.

"That was nice of you to bring out the cider."

Mary waved a dismissive hand. "It's tradition."

One, Faith knew, they hadn't observed in recent years.

"I was telling little Hannah that one of my favorite drinks this time of year is hot apple cider." Mary's lips curved. "She told me she'd never tasted it. I thought she was kidding, but then Charlotte insisted she hadn't had it before either."

Faith grinned. "Which meant you had to make it."

"I wanted to do it. For them. And for the volunteers." Mary chuckled and shook her head. "I put cinnamon candy canes in the ones I gave the twins. That was hands down their favorite part of the drink."

"What did they think of the cider?"

"I believe the consensus was 'not as good as peppermint hot chocolate.'"

"May I interrupt for a moment?"

Faith had been so focused on her conversation with Mary she hadn't noticed Graham's approach.

"You're not interrupting." Mary bestowed a sweet smile on the man. "We were just discussing your lovely daughters."

Graham's attention shifted to a smaller ball of snow that was forming on the huge mound. The twins, along with other children, were busy adding handfuls of the white stuff on what would end up being Frosty's belly.

"I have a few calls I need to make, but I can't leave the girls unattended." He hesitated. "I know you watched them while I was at the market, but if you could—"

He appeared so uncomfortable making the request that Faith rushed to reassure him. "It's no problem. Really. I'll be outside anyway."

"Thank you." Relief skittered across his face. "If they get too rowdy, or you need to send them upstairs, don't hesitate."

"What are you working on?" Though she was simply curious, the second the question left her lips, Faith realized it sounded nosy. She lifted her hands. "Forget I asked. None of my business."

"I'm an ad executive for 45North." Graham named an agency considered one of the top ones in New York. "I'm working on an ad campaign for Dustin Bellamy and Krista Ankrom. They have that new hit television show—"

"I love their show." Mary's eyes brightened.

"It's so..." Faith searched for a word, but came up with only one. "Them."

Last year, Krista—a former supermodel—and Dustin—a former NHL hockey star—had followed in Chip and Joanna Gaines's footprints. Dustin and Krista's new series showcased their relationship as well as touting the work of artisans across the country.

"Dustin and Krista live here part of the year. In fact, they're helping us here today," Faith explained at his curious look, then glanced around. "Their sons are over there helping to build the snowman. Jaxon and Jett are twins and about the same age as your girls."

Graham froze, standing as still as Frosty.

Faith smiled. "They're simply the best couple, so genuine."

"I only met them briefly."

"This will be your chance to get better acquainted," Faith told him.

"I didn't realize they spent time here." That, Graham realized, had been part of the problem with his ad campaign. He had studied the press kit the couple's publicist had provided, but he should have done more research on his own.

"Dustin and Krista are very careful not to publicize their trips to Holly Pointe. They like their family to have some private space." Before he could say anything, Faith called out to a couple adding lights to a weathered wagon filled with buckets of spruce trees.

The two figures straightened, and she caught their eyes. When she motioned them over to the porch, they set down the lights.

"Tell them hello from me." Mary wrapped her arms around herself. "I'm getting chilled. I'm going to step inside for a minute."

Graham watched in disbelief as the celebrity couple strode toward them.

Faith patted his arm. "You're going to find forging these close connections is one of the best things about a small community."

Graham studied the couple as they drew close. He'd seen them earlier helping to build the snowman, but hadn't recognized them. Of course, the last time he'd seen them had been across a conference table in an office overlooking the Manhattan skyline.

That day, they'd been dressed for business. Their expressions had been open and friendly, and they'd paid close attention during his presentation.

After their television show had become a hit, online sales of the folksy items they featured on the show soared. The success had led the couple to look at opening a store in the South that would carry items made by the individual artisans.

Graham had viewed the ad campaign for the brick-and-mortar store as a slam dunk. After he'd finished with the slick presentation, the couple had exchanged a glance, then shaken their heads instead of offering accolades.

What had Dustin said? Ah, yes: *It's an excellent campaign, but not for our store.*

Apparently, Graham had missed the "feel" of their brand by a country mile. Knowing he'd been caught with his pants down had been humiliating. He'd made a rookie mistake and lost their confidence. Now he had thirty days to earn it back.

If he didn't, the partnership he'd been working toward at the ad agency would disappear faster than a snowman in Miami.

"Dustin. Krista." Faith held out both hands as the two

approached. "Thank you for helping today."

"We wanted to be here." Dustin squeezed one of her hands and brushed a kiss across her cheek before casting a curious glance at Graham.

It took a moment, but by the time Krista stepped back from embracing Faith, recognition dawned in Dustin's eyes.

"Graham Westfall." Puzzlement replaced the recognition. "What are you doing here?"

"My daughters, ah, their grandmother—Ginny Blain—lives in Holly Pointe. We came to spend the holidays with her."

"Because Ginny's son and his family are also in town, Graham and his daughters are staying with us," Faith added.

Krista's dark brows drew together. Even though she was ten years beyond what was considered the prime age in the modeling world, Krista's flawless face still looked like it belonged on the cover of a magazine.

Her eyes, a startling blue, fixed on him. "Is your wife with you?"

"My wife passed away three years ago." Graham kept his tone matter-of-fact.

"I'm so sorry." Krista's hand touched his arm, and her eyes filled with sympathy. "I can't imagine."

Dustin shook his head and glanced at his wife.

"It's nice your daughters can spend time with family at this time of year," Krista said. "How old are they?"

"Just turned five. Identical twins."

"I didn't realize you have twins." Krista's smile widened and lit up her face.

Graham pointed. "Those two, the ones getting more snow on themselves than on the snowman."

"Our boys are six." Dustin slid an arm around his wife. "Boundless energy."

"Oh my, yes." When she leaned her head against her husband in a gesture of intimacy, Graham fought a pang of envy.

He remembered when Steph had gazed at him the way Krista looked at Dustin.

"Graham told me the two of you met in New York. On an ad campaign," Faith ventured.

Tall and broad-shouldered, Dustin had an arresting face that spoke of strength and determination. The easy smile on his lips never wavered. "Graham is going to give us the perfect campaign for the store we'll open next summer. It's a challenge. We want something that not only reflects us and our values, but will drive business to the store."

"I'm sorry you have to work on it during the holidays," Krista told him. "But we need—"

Graham held up a hand. "I'm enjoying it. And watching how you two interact with your children and others in the community is giving me a better sense of who you are and the feel I want to see reflected in the ads."

"It's a great town." Dustin grinned. "Faith has probably told you about the skating that's coming up at Star Lake. Santa will arrive, then later the Christmas tree in the town square will be lit."

Krista nodded. "It's great fun. Last year, it was during Thanksgiving weekend."

"It got pushed back to its normal weekend this year." Faith lifted her hands, let them fall. "The earlier time last year was a trial."

"Lucky timing for you and the girls," Krista told Graham. "Santa's arrival is a big hit with the kids."

As the four of them talked, Graham realized that getting to know Dustin and Krista better would aid him in capturing their "vision" for the store.

He had several people to thank for the unexpected gift.

Graham slanted a glance at Faith. Once they were alone, he'd make sure she knew how much he appreciated all she'd done for him.

# CHAPTER FOUR

Graham climbed down from the ladder in the parlor and glanced upward. "Much brighter."

"Having you here is a lifesaver." Mary beamed at him from where she sat across the room doing her embroidery. "Unclogging the kitchen sink and now replacing the light bulb. I'll be sad to see you go."

"We like it here." Hannah looked up from the brightly colored ponies she and her twin were playing with on the rug.

"I'm not leaving." Charlotte didn't even look up, just kept her pony galloping across the floor.

Faith, who'd been standing in the doorway, strolled to the ladder. She'd become very safety conscious after caring for Mary and saw an accident waiting to happen.

"I can take it out to the carriage house." Graham's hand closed around the ladder just as she reached for it.

Their fingers touched, and a sizzle of electricity traveled up her arm. It was a pleasant feeling, and Faith didn't immediately end the contact.

Neither did he.

"It's awkward for one person to handle alone." Conscious that the twins—and likely Mary, too—were listening, Faith smiled and reluctantly pulled back her hand. "We can work as a team. I'll take the front. You take the back."

"I want to help." Charlotte jumped to her feet.

"Me, too." Hannah picked up a pony Charlotte had knocked over and righted it before standing.

"You can definitely help." Faith spoke quickly when she saw the refusal forming on Graham's lips. "We'll need someone to open the door to the carriage house."

"You'll need your coats," Graham told his daughters.

"You and I will need ours, too." Faith tapped his chest in a playful gesture that she immediately regretted.

It felt like she was flirting. Was she flirting? It was difficult to know. She was a friendly person and—

She decided not to worry about it. Graham was here for a month, then he'd be gone.

They'd barely returned and hung up their coats when a knock sounded at the door.

Mary frowned from her position in the rocker near the fire. "I wonder who that could be."

This was their last quiet night at home. Tomorrow, the Candy Cane Christmas House would officially open.

It would be a busy day, Faith knew, with skating at the lake and then candy-making at the house.

"I'll get it, Mary," Faith said when a knock sounded for the second time.

Graham sat on the floor, playing a board game with the twins in front of the fire. From the expressions of startled pleasure on their faces when he'd asked if he could play, having him join them wasn't a frequent occurrence.

Faith glanced down at her fleece-lined leggings topped with an oversize long-sleeved shirt that displayed Rudolph's fluffy red nose. While she wouldn't win any fashion awards, she was comfortable.

Opening the door, she felt a smile blossom on her face at the sight of Ginny holding a plate of peanut brittle.

"Is it too late to pay a visit?" Ginny asked.

Faith hated seeing the tentative look in Ginny's eyes and the two lines of worry on her brow.

"It's never too late for you." Faith injected an extra heartiness into her voice as she ushered the woman inside. "Let me take your coat."

"Did I hear Ginny?" Mary called out from the parlor.

"Yes," Faith called back, hanging Ginny's wool jacket on the coat tree.

They hadn't even stepped into the parlor when Graham appeared. "This is a nice surprise."

Graham held out his hands to his mother-in-law. Ignoring them, Ginny enfolded him in a hug.

Faith's heart swelled in her chest, and she had to clear her throat before she could speak. "She brought us peanut brittle."

It was an inane thing to say, but the look of joy in the twins' eyes when they spotted their grandmother had her mind on pause while her heart took over.

The girls rushed at her, both calling out, "Gramma!"

This time, it was Ginny who had to clear her throat. When she turned in Faith's direction, Faith saw tears shimmering in her eyes.

It had to be difficult, she thought, for her to see two girls who looked so much like their mother. With their honey-blonde hair, big blue eyes and wide mouths, they were the spitting image of Stephanie.

"Daddy let us hang a candy cane on the mem-ry tree." Charlotte pointed. "He said Mommy loved candy canes."

Ginny's gaze shifted to Graham. Her lips trembled before she steadied them and flashed a bright smile in the direction of the twins. "They were her favorite candy. Your mom would be so happy that you thought of her."

Faith had noticed the girls each hanging a different candy cane on the memory tree earlier, but the significance hadn't registered.

"Steph has missed so much," Graham murmured. "I've tried to keep her memory alive by showing them photos and talking about her, but I worry she's just a woman in pictures to them."

"They don't remember her at all?" Faith asked in the same low voice, as the twins explained the game they'd been playing to Ginny.

"Every time the scent of lavender is in the air, Charlotte insists that's how her mother smelled and says she remembers being tucked in at night and kissed on the cheek."

"What about Hannah?"

"She says she remembers her mother's laugh."

"Those are good memories."

"Tiffany, our nanny, is the one who fills the mother role for them now. I've been lucky. Unlike my friends who've gone through nanny after nanny, Tiff has stuck with us."

Ginny kept one arm around each girl, beaming.

After giving Ginny ample time to greet her granddaughters, Mary crossed the room to her dear friend. "This is a special treat. I'm so happy you stopped over."

"I didn't want to intrude—"

"You're family." Faith's comment, spoken with an undisguised genuineness, had Ginny relaxing. "Can I get you some tea? Or maybe hot apple cider?"

"Cider would be wonderful." Ginny's tone turned teasing. "You know my weaknesses."

"That's why I'm going to add a cinnamon stick to the cup." Faith's eyes twinkled as she turned to Graham. "Can I get you a cup?"

"I'm fine." Graham watched Faith head toward the kitchen, her bunny slippers padding against the floor.

It struck him as odd that this could feel so right. The houses he'd grown up in had been nothing like this. At the end of the day, his father and whoever his stepmother was at the time would have never thought to unwind with something as mundane as apple cider.

Bourbon on the rocks had been his father's drink of choice. The steps—there had been three during his childhood—had had varying tastes. He didn't recall much about Sylvia, the one who'd moved in after his mother had taken off when he was six, other than her propensity for Cosmos. The frothy pink drink had been such a strange contrast to the amber liquid of his father's bourbon.

Charlotte pointed to the Sneaky Snacky Squirrel board sitting atop the Persian rug. "Will you play with us?"

When Ginny hesitated, Graham gestured. "That's my log. You can take over for me. Although, full disclosure, there aren't many acorns in my log, so you'll be starting at a disadvantage."

"Are you sure—?"

He smiled at Faith as she returned with a cup for not only Ginny, but one for him as well. "I'm going to sit on the sofa and enjoy my cider."

Despite the odd outfit, Faith looked pretty tonight. Her light brown hair tumbled loose around her shoulders. Two sparkly reindeer clips kept the silky strands back from her face.

Though she wasn't classically beautiful the way Stephanie had been, Faith possessed a kind of beauty that was all her own.

"Thank you for this," Graham said to Faith when she handed him the cup. "I appreciate it."

Their eyes met and locked, and he found himself drawn into her soft-brown depths. The attraction that stirred surprised him, just like it had when their hands had brushed.

How long had it been since he'd felt anything for any woman? He'd been head over heels in love with his wife.

Though he'd dated several women after Steph's death, most of the time the date had been nothing more than taking a plus-one to a business function. Between the long hours he put in for his job and the twins, there wasn't time for romance.

Besides, there hadn't been anyone who'd captured his attention. Even women who, on the surface, appeared to be a perfect match hadn't provoked the kind of feelings Faith brought to the surface.

Perhaps he was simply tired, or—

"Your mother loved board games," he heard Ginny say. "She was really good at them."

"What games did she like?" Charlotte asked, an eagerness in her voice that he heard more often now whenever he brought up Steph.

His mother-in-law began regaling the girls with tales of old-time board games and their mother's prowess. Graham's gaze sought Faith's. Her smile made him feel better, though what he had to feel better about, he wasn't certain.

Maybe it was hearing Ginny talk about his wife and knowing he wasn't the only one who remembered Steph. As the only girl in a family of boys, she had always had a special bond with her mother. While Steph often grumbled that her mother didn't understand the pressure she was under, being an up-and-coming architect in a firm dominated by men, when she'd become pregnant, she and her mother had been on the phone daily.

When Steph had been admitted with preeclampsia, Ginny had flown to New York and remained at her bedside. Steph's fears about approaching motherhood had been eased by Ginny's presence and support.

Graham knew Ginny had once feared he and Steph might never have children because of their focus on their careers. Parenthood had been something they'd both wanted, but in the far, far distant future.

Then, despite being on the Pill, Steph had gotten pregnant. When they learned they were expecting twins, she'd panicked, but he'd assured her they could do this...with the help of a nanny.

The sofa dipped, and Graham turned to see Faith had taken a seat near him. While his mind had been traveling down memory lane, Mary had gotten down on the floor to join the game with Ginny and the girls.

"I haven't seen my grandmother this engaged in…well, I can't remember when." Faith spoke in a low tone, the comment obviously meant for his ears only.

"They all seem to be having a good time." Graham heard the quiver of excitement in Hannah's voice when she announced her log was full.

"Let's play another game." Charlotte reached over and pulled out Candy Land.

Ginny and Mary exchanged glances.

"I'd be up for it." Mary put a hand to her back. "But we need to play at the dining room table. These old bones aren't meant for doing a lot of floor sitting."

"That works for me." Ginny cast a questioning glance in Graham's direction when the girls squealed and hopped to their feet.

Graham lifted a cup that still contained a good amount of cider. "You go ahead. I'm going to sit here in front of the fire while you ladies play."

"I'll keep Graham company," Faith said when their gazes shifted to her.

"Thank you." Ginny called over her shoulder as Hannah took her hand and pulled her into the dining room.

"What was she thanking you for?" Faith asked.

"Time alone with the girls." Graham took a long sip of cider. "It's nice when we're all together, but when I'm there, she has to share the girls with me. The one-on-one time is precious to her."

"She's lucky you two have such a good relationship."

Graham raised a brow.

"Her daughter is gone. Some men might not be so eager to stay in touch."

"Steph was her only daughter. They were close. I like Ginny and want the girls to know her. My father isn't much interested in being a grandfather, so she's really all they have."

"What about your mother?"

"She and my dad divorced when I was six. She left me with him." He shrugged. "Linnea has a new family. To her, I'm a reminder of a marriage that didn't work out."

"I'm sorry."

"Don't be." He shrugged. "I only saw her a handful of times growing up. It isn't as if she was ever a huge part of my life."

Though his tone was matter-of-fact—hadn't he said these same words thousands of times through the years?—a coldness filled his body.

Faith's hand over the one he'd rested on the sofa brought a surge of heat. She gave his hand a gentle squeeze, and when he glanced at her, she offered a tentative smile.

He found himself smiling back. "It isn't what I'd have chosen."

"Life can be like that."

"What about you?" Graham had learned over the years that the quickest way to get off the hot seat was to ask the other person about themselves. "Tell me about your family."

Faith's smile slipped just a little.

*There's a story there,* he thought, and wondered just how honest she'd be. Or would she, like him, gloss over the difficult stuff?

"My father is a cardiologist, my mother a researcher. I have three brothers, all successful. One, like my father, is a physician, only his specialty is oncology. Bryce is an attorney and has his own firm. Evan, well, I already told you about him. Then there's me."

"You're a business owner." Graham had heard Mary talk about Faith's shop, but hadn't had a chance to swing by there.

"Oh, are you referring to my little hobby?" Faith's tone turned mocking, and a bitterness underscored the words.

"Is it a hobby?" Graham kept his expression even as he tried to figure out what was going on.

"No, it's a business. One that, after only two years, is already showing a profit."

He took a sip of cider. "Then why call it a hobby?"

"That's how my family sees it." Faith gave a little laugh and appeared to brush away the melancholy. "I shouldn't let it bother me. Occasionally, their dismissal gets into my head. Either I feel sad or angry, or sometimes both. Which is ridiculous, because I'm doing what I love, so whatever anyone else thinks shouldn't matter."

"Parents have a way of getting into our heads." Graham downed the rest of the cider as if it were a glass of scotch.

"Your dad has expectations?"

"You could say that." Graham wondered how they were back to talking about him. "Being successful is what you do. Above all else. In his head, that's all that matters. When I mentioned I was thinking of selling my New York apartment and getting something smaller and less expensive, you'd have thought I told him I was close to being homeless."

"Why are you thinking of moving?"

There wasn't any judgment in the question, just honest curiosity.

"When it was Steph and me, we were pulling in two good incomes. Now, it's just me with two daughters and a nanny to support."

Faith opened her mouth, then closed it. But he'd been asked the question so many times and in so many ways, he knew what she wanted to know.

"There was no life insurance." Graham tightened his grip on the mug. "We should have had it. We planned to take out policies on both of us once the babies were born. Time got away from us. It was inexcusable."

"Having twins probably kept you busy." There wasn't judgment in Faith's words, but understanding. "Not to mention you probably weren't getting all that much sleep."

Those first two years, the only time Steph had had with her girls, were a blur. Tiffany had helped. Ginny had come down several times and stayed for a couple of weeks. But two infants and busy schedules had equaled chaos. Either he was skipping a meeting to be with them, or Steph was.

"I don't know how we'd have made it through without Tiffany." Graham gazed with unseeing eyes into the fire. "She was a godsend, but unfortunately she couldn't be there twenty-four seven."

"How many weeks did Steph take off once the babies were born?"

"Six."

"Couldn't she have done more under family medical leave?"

"She could have taken up to twelve, but there was no way she'd take that much time off."

"Why not?"

"Her position at her firm was on shaky ground." Knowing the questions poised on Faith's lips had Graham continuing without waiting for her to ask. "It's a firm of mostly men. She had a rough pregnancy with the twins and had to take more time off than she wanted. An important job came up while she was in the hospital with preeclampsia. Overseeing that project went to another associate. She was determined that wouldn't happen again."

"I'd say there are more important things, but I understand."

He cast her a questioning glance.

"Everyone in my family would have done just as she did."

He studied her for a long moment. "Not you?"

"I tried it their way, but that kind of business world isn't for me." She smiled. "We're all different. That's the beauty of life. Wouldn't it be boring if we were all the same?"

"Not according to my father," Graham quipped and made her laugh.

# CHAPTER FIVE

"What a perfect day for ice skating." Sitting on a bench near the edge of the pond, Faith laced up her skates.

"I remember when I came here last year." Stella Johnson glanced over at Faith, her cheeks flushed from the cold. "The temperature was where it is now, and the wind held a bite. Sam and I were just getting acquainted, but when we skated arm in arm, I felt warm."

"You were hot-diggity-hot for him," Mel teased, plopping down on the bench next to Faith. "Even from the Snack Shack, I spotted the sparks."

Stella laughed. "Sometimes that seems so long ago, and sometimes it feels like yesterday."

Stella had come to Holly Pointe to get a story for her Miami newspaper. *Dish the dirt* was what she'd been told by her managing editor. Finding the "dark underbelly" of a town that billed itself as the Capital of Christmas Kindness had been the goal.

Instead of dirt, Stella had fallen in love with the town, the people and with Sam Johnson, who was now her husband.

"What's the latest on the hottie you're living with?" Mel's hazel eyes settled on Faith's.

"Yes." Stella leaned forward. "Tell all."

Faith could feel her cheeks warm despite the cold. "I'm not living with Graham Westfall, and you both know it."

"You're under the same roof," Mel pointed out.

"That's closer than you've been to any guy since I moved to Holly Pointe." Stella glanced at Mel as if seeking confirmation.

Mel nodded. "We want the deets."

Faith glanced around, needing to reassure herself no one was close enough to overhear this ridiculous conversation. "Graham, as you both are well aware, is Ginny's son-in-law. He's here on vacation so his daughters can spend time with their grandmother."

"He's single." Stella wiggled her brows.

"You're under the same roof," Mel intoned for what felt like the thousandth time. "And he's hot."

"Nothing is happening between us," Faith insisted, figuring now wasn't the time to bring up how much she liked the scent of his cologne or the way the skin around his eyes crinkled when he smiled…or how the heat in her belly flared whenever he glanced her way.

Any of those comments would only add fuel to a fire already flaring to life and fanned by her friends' speculative looks.

"If you're not interested..." Mel moistened her lips with the tip of her tongue. "I could—"

"I didn't say I'm not interested." The words popped out before Faith could stop them.

"We knew it." Stella exchanged a look with Mel.

Then, to Faith's horror, the two exchanged high fives.

"What are you going to do about this attraction?" Mel asked, as if there was actually something Faith could do.

"Nothing."

Mel's brow furrowed. "Why not?"

Faith kept her voice even, ready for the teasing to end. "He's only here for a month. Then he's going back to the city."

"A long-distance—" Stella stopped when Faith shook her head.

"He's got a high-powered career and two girls who take the rest of his free time."

"I guess there's only one thing to do." Mel's tone was matter-of-fact.

Stella nodded agreement.

Faith expelled the breath she hadn't realized she was holding. Finally—at last—they'd seen the light. Even die-hard romantics could see there was no point in getting involved with someone who'd be gone in a month.

"Have a fling."

Startled, Faith couldn't have said at that moment which of her friends had come up with that ridiculous solution. She shifted her gaze from Mel to Stella and saw that both appeared not only in agreement but totally serious.

"I can't have a fling." Faith waved a dismissive hand in the air, sending the bells on her new reindeer mittens jingling.

"If you don't remember how, I can give you some pointers," Stella offered.

Mel jerked her head toward Stella. "Her, ah, experience in that area—being a newlywed and all—would be more recent than mine."

"I don't need, nor want, lessons," Faith hissed.

"I thought you knew how to skate." Faith glanced up and saw Mel's brother, Derek, standing before them, a puzzled look on his face.

Derek was a handsome guy, with sandy-colored hair and green eyes. A well-regarded contractor in the area, he was single. Even though she loved green eyes, Derek didn't make her heart beat the slightest bit faster.

For a second, Faith wondered what Mel's brother would say if she told him they hadn't been talking about skating lessons but, rather, bedroom lessons.

She settled for smiling. "I do know how to skate. Stella and Mel were just teasing me."

"Now that you've confirmed I won't have to haul you up from the ice a zillion times, would you care to skate with me?" He held out his hand, and Faith let him pull her to her feet.

No spark.

"I thought you'd be skating with Mandy," Faith said as they started a circle around the lake.

"She isn't here yet," Derek told her. "Besides, I wanted to ask you what the chamber has planned for business owners this spring."

Faith exhaled a relieved breath. Derek had been dating Mandy off and on for the past couple of months, so Faith hadn't thought he was interested in her. Still, she felt better knowing that him asking her to skate was strictly business.

As president of the chamber of commerce, Faith had an inside track on what was going on in Holly Pointe. But, really, there were no secrets in this town. "The annual business Spring Fling is—"

"Hey, there's Mandy." Derek gave Faith's arm a squeeze, then left her, making a beeline across the ice toward the pretty brunette.

Faith continued to skate, debating if she should head over to the Snack Shack for some hot cocoa before Santa arrived and everything got crazy.

"Looks like your partner deserted you."

The unexpected voice had her stumbling. She might have taken a tumble if Graham hadn't grasped her arm and steadied her.

"Wh-what partner?"

"The guy you were skating with." Graham gestured with his

head in Derek's direction as they began to skate, his arm around her waist.

She considered telling him she was steady and he could release his hold, but she liked the closeness too much to end it. "Derek is my friend Mel's brother. He's also a local contractor. He wanted to discuss a business festival that takes place in the spring."

Puzzlement filled Graham's eyes. "He thought you'd know because you're also a business owner."

It might have been a statement, but Faith heard the underlying question. "I'm also president of the chamber of commerce."

Because she was looking at him, Faith saw the startled look that crossed his face.

"I thought you didn't like business stuff."

Had she said that? Or had something she'd said given him that impression?

Faith lifted one shoulder in a shrug. "I'm not into the high-powered stuff, but I enjoy being involved."

"You surprise me, Faith Pierson." The warmth in his green eyes sent the blood flowing through her veins like warm honey.

"Sometimes I surprise myself." She grinned. "Where are the girls?"

"With Uncle Shawn and the cousins."

Faith glanced in the direction he indicated and saw Shawn and his teenage sons teaching the wobbly girls to skate.

Graham must have seen the question in her eyes, because he added, "I planned to teach them, but they don't get much of a chance to interact with family. Shawn and the boys are good skaters."

"You skate pretty well."

"Thank you for noticing." He shot her a wink. "Chelsea Piers is my rink."

She shook her head in disbelief. "No way. I considered that my rink when I lived in the city."

"You're kidding me." He nearly stopped skating as he stared at her. "You lived in Manhattan?"

"In Chelsea," she told him. "When I worked for Benton Lewis."

"That's one of the top accounting firms in the city." He studied her as they rounded the ice, avoiding a group of teenage girls doing figure eights in the center. "What was your position?"

"Senior account analyst."

"Really?"

"I have an MBA from Rutgers."

When Faith thought back to the years that she'd spent climbing the corporate ladder and following her parents' dreams, it felt like another life...or maybe a bad dream.

The second the thought flashed, she shoved it aside. She firmly believed every experience, good or bad, molded you into the person you were. Those years in the corporate world had taught her that, while she loved numbers, she wasn't meant to sit behind a desk.

In fact, she wasn't meant for the corporate world at all.

"How'd you end up in Holly Pointe running your own business?"

Lost in memories, she blinked at the question that seemed to come from far away and took a deep breath.

It was the wrong move if she was hoping to clear her brain. The enticing scent of his cologne flooded her senses and had every nerve ending in her body snapping to attention.

"I told you how I came here to care for my grandmother when she got sick and never went back."

"You just up and left your old life behind?"

The incredulity in his voice reminded her of Thomas. Only after all this time she was able to look back and understand a little more his shock and his attempts to make her see "reason." At the time, she'd been convinced he was thinking only of himself. She now understood her decision to leave everything behind—including him—had been a shock.

"My roommate had moved out the month before. Our lease was up, and I'd found another place, but hadn't committed, so that wasn't an issue." Faith tightened her hold on his sleeve, finding comfort in the touch. "I took a leave from work and told them my grandmother required continued care. They were understanding. My boyfriend, not so much."

Their heads both turned at the same time in the direction of children's laughter. Charlotte and Hannah were up on their skates and making their way slowly around the ice.

Charlotte lifted her hand to wave and slipped, setting off more gales of laughter.

Faith and Graham waved to both girls, and Faith wondered if she should suggest he skate with his daughters.

"What happened with the guy? Are you still in touch?"

"No. I heard from mutual friends that he married last summer." Faith remembered that when she'd heard the news, she hadn't felt anything.

"Did you try to do the long-distance thing?"

She shook her head. "Our relationship had been treading water for some time."

"Making those kinds of decisions is never easy."

"Thomas didn't understand when I told him I needed to come here to care for my grandmother."

"He didn't think you should come?"

"He told me I should hire a professional, an RN or LPN, to care for her." Disappointment flooded Faith now, the same as it had when Thomas had mentioned hiring a nurse the first time. "He wasn't close to his family, so I'll give him a pass. Even my own parents agreed with him. There's a special bond between me and my grandmother. When I came to see her, I was shocked by how weak she was...and even worse, she seemed to have lost her spirit."

"I understand where he was coming from." Graham spoke slowly, as if wanting to be completely honest. "I may have made the same suggestion in his place. But I envy the closeness you share with your grandmother and believe a person has to do whatever feels right to them."

"I haven't regretted it," Faith told him. "Not one single day—"

The clang of a bell split the air, and the exodus from the ice began.

"What's going on?" Graham asked, his brows pulled together in confusion.

"Santa is coming." Faith grabbed his arm and pulled him across the ice at breakneck speed. "You'll want to be with the twins when they see him come over the hill."

Soon after, they reached the edge of the lake and removed their skates. Faith lost track of Graham when she paused to speak with one of her employees, and he continued in search of his daughters.

A minute later, Faith smiled when she saw him with Charlotte and Hannah. He was holding their hands and gazing at where a sleigh, pulled by actual reindeer, crested a nearby hill.

Her heart filled to overflowing when she saw him scoop each girl up into his arms—no easy feat—so they could see over the crowd.

A fling with a single dad of two?

No way was that happening, Faith told herself. No matter how green his eyes.

# CHAPTER SIX

After listening to the twins proclaim that this was the *bestest day ever* for the thousandth time, Graham tucked them into bed. He kissed them on the forehead, then went to work on the ad campaign for Dustin and Krista.

When they'd asserted he'd missed the mark with his first campaign, he'd nodded, accepting the criticism, while trying to decipher what exactly they meant. He'd studied their backgrounds—her career as a supermodel, his awards and accolades as an NHL hockey star.

After retiring from their respective careers, the power couple had brought their images and positive press to a business promoting local artisans in communities throughout the United States. Their television show featured these entrepreneurs and their products.

Their success had led them to the decision to open a brick-and-mortar store in Gatlinburg, Tennessee. A store that would sell items featured on their show.

The store was set to open next summer, and Graham had been tasked with coming up with a knock-it-out-of-the-park ad campaign. The head of the agency and Dustin's father went way back. That was likely the only reason the agency hadn't been kicked to the curb when Graham failed to deliver a satisfactory campaign.

After Dustin and Krista had left the meeting, he'd asked his boss where he'd gone wrong, but Len had had no answers. Graham could tell that his boss was as puzzled as he was, but also worried. In business, friendship and loyalty went only so far. If their agency—translation: Graham—couldn't deliver what Dustin and Krista wanted, the power couple would take their millions somewhere else.

Graham worked on a new campaign for nearly two hours, then ended up scrapping it all. He told himself that he'd go downstairs, grab a piece or two of the homemade fudge in the kitchen, then try again.

When he reached the main floor, he walked softly, not wanting to wake either Faith or her grandmother. A single light blazed in the parlor.

"What are you doing up?"

The voice came from the sofa positioned in front of a fire that was now only embers.

After his heart rate settled, he crossed the room to Faith. "Is that fudge?"

She gestured to the plate sitting on a side table. "Help yourself. I've already had two pieces, which is one too many."

He noticed an empty wineglass next to the plate. "Fudge and wine. A stellar end-of-the-evening snack."

"Especially when paired with a fire." She gestured to the hearth with one hand. "And gently falling snow."

It wasn't the chocolate or the wine or even the large white flakes he could see out the front window that captivated Graham. It was Faith's beautiful face illuminated in the lamp's golden glow.

Something inside Graham stirred. A longing that had been buried had suddenly sprung to life. "Mind if I join you?"

"I'd like that." She motioned to a cabinet with beveled-glass door fronts. "There are glasses in there. This wine goes perfectly with chocolate."

Retrieving a glass, he splashed some wine from the bottle sitting out, then took a seat on the sofa, careful to keep an appropriate amount of distance between them. When he turned toward her, Graham told himself to keep it friendly.

Still, his gaze was drawn to her mouth, to those full sensual lips.

He took a gulp of wine. "This reminds me of a scene out of a movie."

Instead of taking off and running with the comment, she broke off a bite of fudge and popped it into her mouth.

"After the noise and activity of the city, this is an abrupt change," he added.

She lifted a brow. "A welcome one?"

He thought for a moment. Graham knew lots of people, worked with lots of people, who had the social patter down to an art. They talked a lot, but said nothing. He preferred, whenever possible, to speak from the heart. "It hasn't yet been forty-eight hours since we arrived, so the jury is still out."

Surprise flickered across her face. Had she expected that he'd instantly fall in love with the place?

"Too much quiet?" she asked.

"It hasn't been all that quiet."

His comment had her chuckling.

"It's just different." He lifted the wineglass. "I envisioned being at Ginny's, and instead I'm here."

"How did you think things would be at Ginny's?"

Graham broke off a piece of fudge and followed it with a sip of wine. "You were right. I'm not normally big on fruity wines, but this," he glanced at the label, "really does complement the rich chocolate."

"I'm somewhat of an expert on wines."

His gaze sharpened, and he got the feeling there was a lot of things still to uncover about this woman. There were depths to her yet to be plumbed.

"You didn't answer my question." She gazed at him over the rim of her glass. "How did you think things would be at Ginny's?"

"I know Holly Pointe goes all out for Christmas. I was prepared for all the craziness."

Her lips twitched, but she remained silent.

"I hoped the girls would get to know their grandmother on a deeper level than is possible during her short visits to the city." Graham twisted the wineglass back and forth between his thumb and forefinger. "Now, we're not even under the same roof, and Ginny is having to divide her time between Shawn and his family and us."

"Ginny will make time for you and the twins. She—"

"--is an amazing grandmother.," Graham interrupted. "And me, well, I'm determined the girls will have a wonderful Christmas, even if I have to work some of the time."

"I'm confident the twins will love being here. And so will you. Just give yourself time to feel settled." Faith's red lips curved upward. "Trust me, you'll discover this community embraces the Christmas spirit like no other."

Graham took a sip of wine. "It sounds as if you speak from personal experience."

The laugh that came from Faith's lips reminded him of bells jingling. "I'd spent time in Holly Pointe during December as a child. My family would swoop in for several days near Christmas, but we never stayed long. I always felt the magic, embraced it. But once I moved here—"

The flush in her cheeks and the brightness in her eyes were utterly charming.

"What happened when you moved here?" he prompted.

"Let me set the stage." Faith put down her glass and lifted both hands as if ready to paint him a visual picture. "My grandmother had pneumonia, made worse by her not seeking medical attention in a timely manner."

Graham didn't know Mary well, but sensed her independent spirit. He could see her brushing aside symptoms as something that would resolve on their own with time.

Steph had been like that, always healthy and able to push through any virus or bacteria that dared come her way. Which was why the issues she'd experienced during her pregnancy had been so difficult to bear.

The complications had been something that she couldn't simply power through. Taking off time from work, though necessary, had been particularly onerous.

"—in early November."

Graham realized with a start that while his mind had wandered, Faith had continued to speak. He refocused his attention on her.

"She was in far worse shape than anyone in the family realized." Faith pressed her lips together. "She'd lost nearly ten pounds. Weight she didn't have to spare. Despite the meds, she coughed continuously, which sapped her strength. During those first weeks, my goals were simple. I would make nourishing meals and see she got her rest and took her medicine as ordered."

"You didn't get out much."

She chuckled and shook her head. "Not for those first weeks. Besides, going out didn't really appeal to me. The winter that year was one of the worst on record. I swear it snowed every day."

Graham wasn't sure where she was going with this, but if she was trying to build a case for Holly Pointe magic, she was failing miserably. "Didn't you go stir crazy?"

"Friends of my grandmother came to visit. Mel—my friend Melinda Kelly—and her mom, Rosie, brought amazing casseroles to tempt my grandmother's appetite." Faith smiled as if recalling the memory brought back pleasant feelings. "They'd stay, and we'd play cards or board games."

He shook his head and popped another piece of fudge into his mouth. "Completely foreign to me."

She cocked her head. "Which part?"

"Neighbors bringing food. Staying home and playing cards and board games." He thought back to his life in the city, pre-pregnancy. "Before the twins, Steph and I were always on the go. Parties, dinners out, job functions."

"I know that life." She gave a little laugh. "I lived that life. It works for a lot of people. Like you, they can't imagine different. But when I came here—"

She stopped herself, waved a hand. "I digress. By Thanksgiving, I'd settled into life in Holly Pointe. When my grandmother accused me of hovering, I started making things in the woodshop my grandpa used out back. Nothing big. Pieces of wood that I painted with inspirational messages, to start. Corny as it sounds, doing those activities soothed my soul."

"It doesn't sound corny." The look on her face held a glow, and whatever peace her soul had found from the activity seemed to radiate from within. "Not at all."

"Winter had come early that year and hit hard. There was already a foot of snow on the ground that first week in November." A smile lifted Faith's lips as she picked up her glass. "But by the time December rolled around, I began to see what life in Holly Pointe was all about. Even though we didn't do the Candy Cane Christmas House that year, friends from the community decorated outside. By that time, with my assistance, my grandmother was able to go out and participate in a few community activities."

Her eyes took on a distant glow.

"You were hooked."

She blinked.

"On Holly Pointe," he added.

"I was." A shadow passed over her face. "I knew then that I wouldn't be returning to New York. Some of it was that, despite the strides she'd made, my grandmother still needed my help. Mostly, it was that this place feels like home in a way that the city never did."

"With your apartment lease being up, you didn't have any loose ends to tie up."

"Only Thomas." Her fingers tightened around the stem of her empty wineglass. She set it down again. "I think I knew it was over when he wasn't supportive of my coming here to help my grandmother. He was still a good guy, and we had some fun times."

"How did he take it?" Graham kept his gaze fixed on her face.

"Better than I thought." Her lips twisted in a wry smile. "I guess he wasn't as into me as I thought. Which was good, I guess."

"Do you keep in touch?"

"No." She shook her head, as if for extra emphasis. "I believe I mentioned that he married this past summer. I'm happy for him."

"Is that something you want for yourself?"

"Sure. Someday. With the right guy." Her gaze drifted to the fire before returning to him. "I'd like a husband and a family. But it has to be right, you know?"

"Not just anyone will do," he quipped.

"Absolutely not." She slanted a glance at him. "What about you? You're young. Do you see yourself marrying again?"

"Maybe." He lifted one shoulder in a slight shrug. "But I have two daughters to think of. We'll be a package deal. So—"

"Not just anyone will do."

He lifted his glass in a mock toast. "Exactly."

The topic moved on to inconsequential things before Faith mentioned Dustin and Krista.

"They're having a party at their house tomorrow night. Since you're working on their campaign, you should go." She offered an encouraging smile. "It would give you a chance to become better acquainted."

"Only one problem," he said.

She arched a brow.

"I wasn't invited." Graham wished he'd received an invitation. The opportunity to see the couple in their natural habitat, interacting with friends, could be invaluable in helping him nail their brand.

If his attempts earlier tonight were any indication, he still didn't have a good feel for what this power couple was all about.

"I was invited." Faith paused. "Don't take this wrong, but you could come as my plus-one."

"Why would I take that wrong?"

She flushed. "I just didn't want you to think I was proposing a date."

"I didn't think that." Graham held her gaze. "Even so, what would be so wrong with a date?"

Faith had wanted to kiss Graham. When those amazing eyes settled on her, the simple look ignited a fire in her belly. It had taken all her restraint not to curl her hands into his shirt and pull him to her.

That raw need confused her. She barely knew the guy. Now, as Faith undressed in the privacy of her room, she mulled over the attraction that flared whenever he was near.

Tonight wasn't the first time she'd found herself wondering what kissing Graham would be like.

It was best—yes, it was best—he'd excused himself to head upstairs to bed.

Was he in bed now?

Was he thinking of her?

Faith told herself it was ridiculous to get moon-eyed over

someone who was just visiting. A man who would soon go back to his fast-paced city life and not give her a second thought.

Still, it had been a long time since Faith had been kissed. Perhaps while Graham was here, they could enjoy each other's company. Maybe even share a kiss.

Just as long as she didn't forget that after Christmas, he'd be gone.

# CHAPTER SEVEN

"Are we there yet?" Charlotte called from the back seat.

Graham resisted a sigh. Hadn't he answered that very same question from her sister less than sixty seconds earlier? He reminded himself they were children and excited about the sleepover at their grandma's house tonight. "We're close. I'll let you know when I see her house."

"We get to sleep in the living room," Hannah told him for the tenth time.

"On *rafts*." Charlotte squealed the word. "Like on an ocean."

Hannah giggled. "I hope there aren't any sharks."

By the excitement in the car, you'd have thought they'd be sleeping in a five-star hotel instead of spending the night on air mattresses.

"Are we there—?" Hannah began.

"The house is in sight." Graham expelled a sigh of relief as the ranch-style home came into view.

He'd barely pulled into the driveway and shoved the car into park when the girls unbuckled their seat belts and hopped out of their boosters. They raced up the freshly shoveled walk to the front door.

"Walk," he called out, feeling like a grinch as joyous laughter rippled back at him.

Ginny must have been waiting for them, because the door opened before the twins reached it. She hugged both girls, then spoke with them briefly before stepping to the side as they shot inside.

Ignoring the brisk wind, Graham grabbed overnight bags before strolling up the walk. The girls had disappeared, but Ginny remained at the door. When he reached her, just as she had with the girls, she wrapped her arms around him.

"Please tell me you can come in for a minute." A hopeful look blanketed her face as she motioned him inside. "Shawn and his family aren't back yet from the slopes, so it's pretty calm. For the moment, anyway."

Her smile had him setting the bags inside the door and deciding to stay for a few.

The bearded collie stood quivering behind Ginny, his large brown eyes fixed on Graham. When Graham smiled at the dog, Beau let out a woof, and the swish of his tail picked up speed.

A startled look flitted across Ginny's face as if she'd forgotten about the animal. She fixed her gaze on the animal. "Beau. Find the girls."

After a momentary hesitation, the dog turned to jog down the hall.

"I'm trying out a new recipe—Nutella hot chocolate." Ginny's tone turned persuasive. "Will you join me for a cup if I promise to keep Beau at bay?"

"I like dogs," he hastened to assure her. "The only reason Steph and I didn't have one was because—"

"You were both so busy."

Graham nodded. As he followed her to the kitchen, he let the warmth and tantalizing smells of chocolate and freshly baked bread wrap around him. "I told Steph once that your house always feels like a home."

"Thank you. That means so much." Tears sprang to Ginny's eyes, but she blinked them back. "How about that cup of cocoa?"

"Sounds good. I—"

"Gramma." Charlotte burst into the kitchen, followed by Beau and Hannah. "We found the prize."

Graham lifted a brow. "Prize?"

"Gramma sent us on a scav-ger hunt," Charlotte explained.

"She gave us a clue." Hannah lifted a single finger. "But just one."

"The dolls were under a blanket," Charlotte announced proudly. "But we found them."

For the first time, Graham noticed a small doll clutched in each girl's hand.

"When I saw the hair sticking out from under the blanket, I screamed." Hannah opened her mouth and emitted an ear-splitting shriek.

"I did, too." Apparently determined not to be outdone, Charlotte opened her mouth.

Graham held up a staying hand. "I get the picture."

"I'm glad you found the dolls." Ginny reached over and gently stroked Hannah's hair. "Your mother loved surprises. She'd have screamed, too."

Charlotte motioned to her sister. "Let's put them on the rafts."

Hannah's eyes brightened. "They can float on the ocean with us."

"The sofa can be an island." Charlotte's voice rose as she grabbed her sister's hand.

Their excited chatter lingered even after they disappeared into the other room.

"They're lovely girls, Graham." Ginny moved to a slow cooker that emitted the rich scent of chocolate. "You're doing a fine job raising them."

Her approval meant a lot, though Graham wasn't sure the

praise was deserved. "Tiffany spends more time with them than I do."

The realization brought a heaviness to his chest.

"Tiffany is a wonderful woman and an exceptional nanny," Ginny said diplomatically as she added a dollop of whipped topping to the cups of cocoa. "But—"

"But..." Graham prompted when she didn't continue.

"But you're their father. They need your guidance and love most of all." Ginny took a seat opposite him at the table. "Trust me. Your years with the twins will go by in a heartbeat."

Graham wrapped his fingers around the mug and let the warmth seep into his hands. "I plan on making changes."

The slower pace of Holly Pointe, and the lack of outside distractions, had given Graham time to assess not only his professional life but his personal one as well.

"Tonight is a good first step."

The cryptic comment had him frowning. "Tonight?"

"Going on a date." Ginny brought the ceramic mug that boasted World's Best Grandmother on the side to her lips.

"It isn't a date," he protested, then stopped himself from saying more. He didn't want Ginny to think he was dissing Faith.

Graham liked Faith. He had fun with her. He had no doubt this would be an enjoyable evening.

"Why isn't it?"

Pulling his attention back to Ginny, Graham realized his mind had wandered. "Pardon?"

"Why isn't going to a party with Faith a date?" Puzzlement filled Ginny's blue eyes. "Don't you like her?"

"Of course I like her. We're friends." Though he hadn't known Faith long, she was a wonderful woman. Quirky, sure, but she had a good heart. "She asked me to attend the party with her so I can get to know Dustin and Krista better."

Graham saw no need to mention the attraction that hovered in the air whenever he was with Faith. Shifting under Ginny's intense scrutiny, Graham tried for casual. "Faith is a wonderful woman with many fine qualities."

Ginny's lips curved as she lifted her cup of cocoa. "You know, it's okay for you to date a wonderful woman with many fine qualities."

"It's not a date," Graham insisted.

"If you say so." Ginny lifted one shoulder in a slight shrug. "I hope you have fun tonight with this lovely woman who isn't your date."

The impish gleam in her eyes had him shaking his head. "Ginny…"

"Graham." She placed her warm hand over his. "Faith is an excellent choice for a friend. All I'm saying is you deserve to have fun. You deserve friends, and I believe one thing we can both agree on is you couldn't find a better friend than Faith."

"The road looks treacherous." Graham glanced out the window as Faith navigated their way up the winding mountain road.

He'd offered to drive, but since she knew the way and had a four-wheel-drive vehicle, it made sense for him to go with her. Besides, wasn't that what he was doing tonight? Going with her as her plus-one?

"Mountain roads can be bad, though the crews do a good job of maintaining them. Dustin and Krista pay Derek to keep the roads leading to their house clear." Even as she spoke, Faith kept her attention firmly fixed on the road ahead.

The car slid slightly, and Graham glanced at Faith.

"Just an ice patch." Her fingers might have tightened ever-so-slightly around the steering wheel, but her voice remained calm and reassuring.

"Not worried at all," he lied. "I know I'm in excellent hands."

A dimple he hadn't even known she possessed winked in her right cheek.

A comfortable silence filled the car. As Faith needed to focus on the road, Graham didn't fill the silence with inane chatter.

He still couldn't believe he was going out on a non-date in his late wife's hometown. Faith had told him that the event was casual, that there would likely be people there wearing ski sweaters and denim.

Graham had settled for dark pants and a sweater. Faith, on the other hand, wore a dress. This one didn't have reindeer on it, but was covered in multiple Santa faces. Some might consider the pattern quirky, but on her, it struck Graham as, well, cute. Her hair was pulled back into a twisty, messy knot and secured with two red chopsticks.

He liked the look, just as he liked her. She was fresh and genuine and fun to be around. She had her own unique style, and he found her sense of independence and seeming ease with everyone incredibly sexy.

She was a breath of fresh drama-free air.

Last night, he'd been tempted to kiss her. Seriously tempted. He'd heeded the warning bells telling him to take a step back. Still, as Ginny had said, there was no reason he and Faith couldn't enjoy each other's company while he was in Holly Pointe.

The paved lot beside the large log home was filled with cars by the time they arrived. Faith found a spot between two massive 4x4 trucks that looked as if they could bench-press a ton.

He took her arm as they made their way to the brightly lit home. It struck Graham that's how he saw the place. Not as a house, but as a home.

From the massive front porch, which he could envision festooned with flowers in the summer, to the large evergreen wreath on the door and the lace curtains at the windows, it all said welcome home.

The woman who opened the door wore black pants, a crisp white shirt and a smile.

"Welcome. Dustin and Krista are with other guests in the great room to your left." She held out a hand. "May I take your coats?"

As they handed over the garments, Faith didn't appear surprised, which meant Dustin and Krista likely often hired help for their parties.

"You're with Creative Creations out of Jay Peak," he heard Faith say as the woman handed Graham a claim ticket.

"I am." The middle-aged woman, her brown hair laced liberally with strands of gray, studied Faith. "Cecelia Odvody. I own the company. One of my employees has strep throat, so I'm filling in. Have we met?"

"Faith Pierson." Faith shot the woman a smile. "We worked together on some signage for an event you were catering."

"Of course. Faith. Now I remember. I'm sorry for not making the connection." The woman rolled her eyes. "My only excuse is it's been rather hectic with Darlee calling in at the last minute. It's good to see you again."

The woman cast a curious glance in Graham's direction, as if wondering if he was someone else she should recognize.

"Cecelia, this is Graham Westfall." Faith placed a hand on his arm. "Graham is Ginny Blain's son-in-law."

"You were Stephanie's husband."

Graham steeled himself against the sympathy in her eyes. "You knew my wife?"

"Steph worked for me a couple of summers in high school."

"I didn't realize she had a job back then."

"She didn't put in a lot of hours," Cecelia told him. "Just enough to buy some pretty clothes and save up for lift tickets."

"That sounds like Steph." He chuckled. "She loved the slopes."

How many times over the years had they planned a relaxing ski vacation only to cancel because of work obligations?

"I ran into Ginny last month at a function we catered." Cecelia smiled. "She was so looking forward to seeing her granddaughters. It was all she could talk about."

"They're at her house tonight for a sleepover." Graham chuckled. "I've been advised not to come by to pick them up until late morning. Apparently, chocolate chip pancakes are on the menu."

Puzzlement furrowed Cecelia's brow. "Ginny said you were going to stay with her."

"That was the plan." Graham kept his tone light. "Shawn and his family are also here for a couple of weeks, so the house was a bit crowded."

"Finding a place can be difficult this time of year." Cecelia cocked her head. "Where are you staying?"

Faith stepped back into the conversation.

"Graham is renting the upstairs at my grandmother's house." Faith cast a teasing glance in his direction. "I warned him it'll be noisy. He took the space anyway."

"You'll love it." Cecelia, apparently hearing footsteps on the porch, offered a quick smile. "Nice seeing you again, Faith. Good to meet you, Graham. Leona, please take the door while I put away these coats."

Leona, an older woman with tight gray curls, smiled pleasantly at him and Faith before stepping around them to greet the next guests.

"Let's find our host and hostess." Faith reached out and took his hand, ostensibly to pull him out of the foyer into the large room filled with laughter and conversation.

Graham's fingers curled around hers, sending a familiar heat shooting through his body.

The spark in her eyes told him Faith felt it, too.

She said nothing, only tugged him into the room, her hand still wrapped in his.

Dustin and Krista spotted them almost immediately. They said something to the couple they were speaking with, then began winding their way across the room to where he and Faith stood.

"Faith." Krista, dressed completely in winter white except for shiny black boots, gave Faith a hug. "You're wearing my favorite dress. But where's the Santa hat?"

Faith returned the hug. "I left it at home."

Krista raised her hand to Faith's hair. "Love the chopsticks."

Graham couldn't miss the genuine warmth between the two women. Though they were as different as night and day, there was a definite connection.

"Graham. I'm happy you could make it." Dustin shook his hand and slapped him on the back.

Dustin looked as fit and healthy as he had during his nine seasons in the NHL. There was no evidence in his stride of the torn ACL that had sidelined his career. As well as no trace of the bitterness that often hung around athletes who'd been forced into early retirement.

If anything, Dustin looked like a man happy and satisfied with the direction his life had taken.

"Faith invited me to come with her. I hope you don't mind." Though Dustin had acted as if Graham had received his own invitation, it was important to Graham that Dustin knew he wasn't crashing.

"Any friend of Faith's is a friend of ours." Dustin flashed a smile in Faith's direction, the one that had made him a favorite of female hockey fans, before refocusing on Graham. "How's the ad campaign coming?"

"Good. It'll be ready for you to preview at the end of the month."

Krista slipped an arm through her husband's. "Don't tell me you're talking business."

Instead of chiding, she had a teasing glint in her eyes.

"Just checking in," Dustin answered.

"This one," Krista gestured with one hand toward her

husband, "is super stoked about the store. I don't think I've seen him this excited since his team won the Stanley Cup."

"Not true." His expression turned solemn.

Her perfectly manicured brows pulled together. "What did I forget?"

"Only the two most important events in my life." He lifted a hand and, with gentle fingers, tucked a strand of dark hair behind her ear. "When we were married and when our boys were born."

Graham didn't quite know what to think when Krista wrapped her arms around her husband's neck and kissed him. He thought of the parties he and Steph had attended. Such a bold display of affection would have been deemed inappropriate.

Dustin grinned.

Krista winked. "There'll be more of that…later."

Looping one arm around his wife, Dustin swept the other arm in a wide gesture. "Both bars offer nonalcoholic options, including a wide variety of soft drinks. I assume one of you is the designated driver."

Faith raised her hand like a schoolgirl in a classroom. "That would be me."

"Good." Dustin's expression turned serious. "Our road and alcohol don't mix well."

Krista tugged on his sleeve. "Sam and Stella just got here."

"Excuse us." Dustin's gaze shifted from Faith to Graham. "Perhaps we'll have a chance to talk more about the campaign later."

"I hope not," Graham muttered under his breath as the couple strolled off.

Faith shot him a concerned look. "Not going well?"

"Not going." Graham shrugged. "It will come. If I don't try to force it."

"It's that way with my products." Faith offered a sympathetic nod. "If I try to force things, a wall goes up. A wall I can't seem to breach. If I relax, take a walk, put my mind on other things, that's when inspiration strikes."

Faith understood the creative process, Graham realized, in a way that most people didn't. People usually acted like creativity was a faucet you could turn on and off at will. Maybe for some it was. Steph, he remembered, never seemed stuck for an idea. It wasn't like that for Graham. He might struggle, but he never gave up.

"I'm hoping," he confided, keeping his voice soft, the words for her ears only, "that being here tonight will give me a better feel for who they are, not just the hype in the media."

"This is who they are, Graham." Faith stepped close and lowered her voice.

The fresh scent he associated with her wafted over him. He inhaled deeply. He'd never have believed the scent of vanilla could be so sensual. So intoxicating.

"For them, home and family are paramount." Her eyes blazed with conviction. The heat stirred something in him. "They also have tons of energy and drive. I'm sure that's why they were so successful in their other careers."

Resisting the urge to pull her close, Graham filed away the information. There were many questions he could have asked about the power couple, but now didn't seem the time or place. The stylish, yet homey feel of the cabin—if you could call a five-thousand-square-foot home a *cabin*—had already given him a stronger understanding of the couple.

As had the display of affection he'd witnessed.

He was off to a good start. Because this was a party Faith had undoubtedly anticipated, he didn't plan to spend the entire night talking about Dustin and Krista. Or his advertising campaign. He wanted Faith to have fun.

"You can feel free to mingle without me," he told her.

Her brows pulled together. "I don't understand."

"I mean, I enjoy being with you, but I'm baggage. I don't know many of these people, while you know everyone." Graham thought of the parties he'd attended with Steph. The parties she'd gone to with him. They'd often separated so the other could work the room. "I don't want you to feel as if you have to babysit me."

"I brought you here because I like being with you."

Her words touched him in a way he didn't want to examine too closely. He told himself she was simply being kind. And generous. She was that kind of woman.

"You brought me here because you thought it would be good for my career to become better acquainted with my clients," he pointed out.

"That, too," Faith admitted. "But if I didn't enjoy your company, I wouldn't have offered."

Their eyes met. For a long moment, neither spoke. A shimmering heat filled the air, broken only when a guest bumped into Faith, sending her lurching into Graham.

He placed steadying hands on her arms, holding her close for a moment longer than necessary.

"Sorry," the person called from behind her.

"No worries," she called back, her eyes never leaving Graham's face. When she finally spoke, her voice was breathy with a teasing lilt. "So, dear baggage for the evening, how about I introduce you around?"

"How 'bout you start with me?" A pretty woman with red hair stepped forward and shot out her hand. "Melinda Kelly."

# CHAPTER EIGHT

With the falling snow blanketing any sounds, the trip down the mountain seemed almost peaceful. It helped that Graham was now confident in Faith's driving abilities and that the tension that had him in a stranglehold on the way up had disappeared.

"Your friend Mel seems nice." Graham saw no need to mention that a single look from Melinda Kelly had felt like a two-hour interrogation.

"She liked you." Faith sounded pleased by the thought.

"How could you tell?" Graham wasn't simply making small talk, he wanted to know. While Mel had been extremely pleasant, Graham had the feeling she'd have been that way even if she'd hated him.

The woman was clearly protective of her friend. Graham admired that quality, even if sensing Mel's sharp and assessing gaze on him during the course of the evening had been a little off-putting.

Faith's impish smile brought with it a rush of warmth. She really did have the best smile, Graham thought. So open and genuine.

"Mel told me." Her tone was matter-of-fact.

Graham was truly perplexed. He and Faith had been at each other's sides the entire evening. Spending that much time with a single person during an event was a new experience for him. One he'd discovered he liked very much.

He suspected most of the reason the evening was so pleasurable was due to Faith. Her upbeat attitude was infectious. And while he noticed she listened more than she spoke, Graham discovered she was extremely well-read and knowledgeable on a wide variety of topics.

"When did she tell you?" Though the answer didn't matter, Graham was curious. He couldn't think of a time they hadn't been together.

"When you went to get me a drink and got caught up in a conversation with Dustin." Faith shrugged. "Mel saw an opportunity and seized the moment."

Ah, that made sense. He'd forgotten about his second conversation with Dustin. Getting better acquainted with the sports star and his wife had been the main reason he'd gone to the party. Or so he'd told himself.

"He seems like a good guy. Very driven."

"I believe Dustin will always be driven. I think you have to have that warrior mentality to succeed in the NHL," Faith mused aloud. "I've seen a change in him the last couple of years, though, with an increased focus on home and family."

"With kids, time goes by so quickly." Graham thought about his conversation with Ginny. Dustin wasn't the only driven man capable of making changes. "When I return to New York, I'm going to spend more time with the girls."

"They'll like that. You'll like it, too." Approval ran like warm syrup, thick and sweet, through her words. Without taking her eyes off the road, Faith reached over and gave his hand a quick squeeze.

There was nothing sexual about the touch, simply one friend showing support to another. Why was it, then, that when Faith touched him, even just a careless brush against his arm or a squeeze of his fingers, it felt like more?

Simply being in the close confines of the car with her, having the scent of vanilla teasing his nostrils, had his body on high alert. She must have freshened her lipstick before they left, because the rich red on her lush mouth was like a siren's call.

Would her lips taste like cherry? Or strawberry? However she tasted, Graham had no doubt her lips would be as sweet as the woman herself.

He slanted a sideways glance and wondered how sweet could be so sexy.

The talk shifted to the weather and to her grandmother, who appeared to be continuing to make remarkable strides this Christmas season. By the time they reached home, and that's how Graham was starting to think of the old Victorian, a watchful waiting filled the car.

Taking Faith's arm—just because the sidewalks were shoveled and salted didn't mean there couldn't be slick spots—they strolled in companionable silence to the darkened house.

Once inside the foyer, she turned to him, face uplifted, eyes dark and luminous.

Hoping he wasn't misreading the signals, Graham tugged Faith to him. She came easily, wrapping her arms around his neck. Her puffy coat might make any real body contact impossible, but she was finally in his arms. That's what mattered.

He cleared his throat, his eyes never leaving hers. "I want to kiss you."

"Good." She smiled. "Because I want to kiss you, too."

He wasn't sure who made the first move, wasn't sure it mattered. All he knew was his lips were on hers, and it felt as if it was meant to be. All of this.

Her in his arms.

His mouth on hers.

The kiss battered his body and soul with power and fury. Lips melded as if fused. His heart raced.

When they finally came up for air, a shaky breath escaped Graham's lips. "Wow."

"I knew it would be like this." Faith brushed another quick kiss across his lips before stepping back. "Thanks for a wonderful evening. And for the amazing kiss."

Before Graham could utter a word, she turned in the direction of her bedroom.

For one crazy second, he considered following her. Until he reminded himself he hadn't been invited.

"You, Faith Pierson, are a mighty temptress," he murmured. "What you do to me…"

Then, realizing what he'd said, he chuckled and headed toward the stairs, shaken and alone.

As Graham drove to Ginny's house the next morning, his mind replayed the events of the previous evening. He'd arrived at the cabin as an outsider, but by the time he'd left, he was part of the group.

It helped that Ginny had lived in Holly Pointe her whole life, and many of those at the party knew her. What seemed to have the greatest impact, though, was that he'd come to the party with Faith. Though she'd lived here for only three years, it was apparent Faith was firmly woven into the fabric of this community.

Graham thought of the kiss that had capped off the evening. Although *kiss* seemed far too tame a word for the explosion of raw want and need that had racked his body.

Had he really wondered if she'd taste like strawberries or cherries? Graham chuckled as he pulled into Ginny's driveway. Once his mouth had met hers, there'd been no time to think or wonder. In that moment, all he'd known was one taste wouldn't be enough.

The thought had him pausing with his hand on the door. He liked Faith, liked her a lot. He wanted to spend more time with her. Wanted to kiss her again. The truth was, he wanted to do a lot more than kiss.

But was that wise? Ginny had made it clear she had no trouble with him spending time with Faith—*dating* Faith—but was that fair to Faith? Was it smart?

Logic told him to slow things down.

Yes, Graham decided, a slowdown would be best. Before he reached the front stoop, the door opened, and the twins rushed out to greet him.

"Where is everyone?" he asked Ginny when he stepped inside, an arm around each girl's shoulders. No way was the house this quiet if Shawn and his family were here.

"Beau is in the backyard, romping in the snow. Shawn, Morgan and the kids are on their way back to Jay Peak for another day of skiing." Ginny's lips curved as if both thoughts gave her pleasure. "I made them breakfast, and they took off about fifteen minutes ago. Can I interest you in a cup of coffee? Or I could rustle you up something to eat?"

Graham hesitated. Today was candy-making in Mary's large commercial kitchen. According to Faith, those who didn't have the knowledge or the room to make candy in their own homes came over for help and camaraderie. Some simply enjoyed doing such activities as a group, rather than alone.

Graham had hoped to quickly pack the girls into the car and make it back to the house before he had to fight his way through a downstairs filled with women. The hopeful look in Ginny's eyes had him changing that plan. "I'd love some coffee."

"Yay." Charlotte gestured with one hand. "While you talk to Gramma, me and Hannah are going to put our ponies on rafts."

Glancing in the direction indicated, he saw the air mattresses now held an array of brightly colored ponies. “Sounds like fun.”

“Gramma made us pancakes.” Hannah tugged on his arm. “With chocolate chips.”

“Is that right?”

“Not just *in* the pancakes,” Hannah emphasized, “but on top, too.”

“Don’t forget the whipped cream.” Charlotte rubbed her tummy. “Yum-my.”

“We had real orange juice that Gramma squeezed herself.” Hannah beamed up at Ginny.

“She said it was Mommy’s favorite breakfast.” Charlotte glanced at Graham as if seeking confirmation.

He cleared his throat. “It was indeed your mommy’s favorite.”

Charlotte smiled. “I told Gramma it was like Mommy was here, watching us eat.”

Graham wasn’t sure what to say to that, so he only nodded.

“Let’s play ponies, Han.” Charlotte grabbed her sister’s hand, but Hannah’s feet remained rooted to the hardwood.

“You’re not leaving without us?” she asked her dad.

“I’m not going anywhere.” He ruffled her hair and felt a surge of love.

“Okay.” She offered him a bright smile. “Just checking.”

Graham followed Ginny into the kitchen he’d been in many times before. Well, maybe not all that many times. When he and Steph were first married, there were so many places they wanted to see.

They’d made it to Holly Pointe a total of two times before Steph got pregnant and not at all after the twins were born.

Ginny had made the trek to the city numerous times, insisting it was easier for one person to travel than for four—and then three—especially when the twins were infants.

Looking back, Graham felt ashamed for so easily accepting Ginny’s largess.

"Have a seat." She waved him to a scarred oak table with a bench on one side and chairs flanking the three other sides. "I'll get you a cup. Do you still like it black?"

"I do." He shook his head. "I've never understood how you remember everyone's coffee preferences."

"Not everyone." She set the steaming coffee in front of him. "Just those important to me."

"Thank you again for keeping the girls overnight." He lifted the cup and took a long sip. Hot and strong, just the way he liked it. "We didn't get back until late and—"

"You don't have to thank me," Ginny interrupted. "It was my pleasure. Did you have a nice time at the party?"

"It was an enjoyable evening."

"You had a nice time with Faith?"

It was apparent that Ginny was fishing for details, but holding back. Graham set down his cup, remembering the kiss. No matter how much he liked Ginny, he really didn't want to discuss his attraction to Faith with his late wife's mom.

Shifting uncomfortably in his seat, Graham considered how to best respond. Though he knew he could count on Ginny to keep any confidences, telling her that he'd kissed Faith was definitely off the table.

"Faith is a gem. She introduced me around and made sure I had a nice evening." When he saw questions forming on Ginny's lips, questions he had no intention of answering, Graham pushed forward. "Living at Mary's is working out just fine. Anytime you want to come over there and be with the twins, or want me to bring them over here, you just say so."

"I'm glad it's working out, but—" Ginny glanced around the small kitchen. "It's times like this I wish my house was as big as Mary's."

"This won't be the only time the girls and I will be back in Holly Pointe." Graham wrapped his fingers around the ceramic mug, welcoming the warmth. "We'll find a time this spring or summer to return."

Hope filled Ginny's eyes. "You mean it?"

"I do." Shame flooded him. He should have made trips back to Holly Pointe more of a priority. For the girls' sake as well as Ginny's.

Graham wanted Ginny to see the twins as much as possible this month. Recalling what was going on at the house today, he smiled. "How are you at candy-making?"

Faith glanced in the bedroom mirror and added a bit more red to her lips. If the way Graham's gaze had lingered on her mouth last night had been any indication, he'd liked her new lipstick.

She touched her fingers to her lips, recalling the moment his mouth had closed over hers. Though she'd been kissed plenty of times, it had never been heart-pounding or the slightest bit soul-searing.

A chuckle rose up and spilled out at the fanciful words. Still, they fit the situation. Would he kiss her again? Or maybe she'd kiss him. The thought made her red lips widen as she stepped out of her bedroom.

Though it was barely nine, the hum of voices and excited chatter filled the downstairs. The Candy Cane Christmas House was officially open for business.

Candymakers of the community had arrived in full force. Today, all sorts of candies would be made, from the standard to the exotic. Peppermint bark? Peanut butter snowballs? Hopefully, there would be some three-chip English toffee, one of Faith's personal favorites.

She wished she could stay and help. But she'd spent too much time away from her business the past few days.

Because the kitchen was a hot spot, Faith knew it'd be foolish to attempt to grab a cup of coffee. Thankfully, her business wasn't far from Rosie's or the Busy Bean...

The second the thought struck, she had to chuckle. Nothing was far from her business in Holly Pointe. Stopping by the kitchen, she surveyed the scene. Her grandmother was there, stirring a pot of chocolate while laughing with Norma.

Faith scanned the room. When she spotted Mel, she let out the breath she hadn't realized she'd been holding. At one time, her grandmother had been able to handle the groups coming in for the various festivities. After the pneumonia, being the only one in charge had become too much for Mary.

Out of love for her grandmother and for what she and the house meant to the community, people signed on to be Mary's "helper" during these December events. Mel was her helper today.

When Mel spotted Faith, she rushed over to give her a hug.

"Looks like everything is under control." Faith gestured to the organized group.

"It's going well." Mel glanced around. Even though no one was within earshot, she kept her voice low. "I enjoyed meeting Mr. Hottie at the party last night. He is adorable."

"He's a good guy." Faith would tell Mel about the amazing kiss later. But not here. Not now.

"Are you going out with him again?" Mel asked.

Faith resisted the urge to touch her lips. "No idea."

Disappointment skittered across Mel's face. "He appeared stuck on you. He barely took his eyes off you all evening."

"I'm that kind of girl." Faith fluffed her hair and batted her lashes. "Men find me irresistible."

Mel laughed. "Are you headed to the shop?"

"I am. Lots to do, but I'm looking forward to it."

Mel smiled. "You found your passion."

"I have." Faith expelled a happy breath. "I'm blessed to be able to do what I love."

Mel gave her a gentle shove. "Get going and enjoy."

"Don't eat all the candy. Leave some for me."

Mel's smile turned sly. "No promises."

Faith's coat was on, and she was nearly to the front door when it swung open. The fact that someone was coming in without ringing the bell didn't surprise her. Not with the Come on In signage on the porch.

But her heart skipped a beat at the sight of the dark-haired man. "Graham."

Not just Graham, she realized, but Hannah, Charlotte and Ginny.

Faith gave Ginny a hug. "It's good to see you." Then she turned to the girls. "Where have you been? I've missed you."

It was an exaggeration, of course. She'd seen them twelve hours earlier, right before Graham had taken them to Ginny's to spend the night.

"We were at Gramma's," Hannah said, all serious.

"We slept on rafts." Charlotte, not to be outdone, stepped forward. "And played with Beau."

"Do I know Beau?" Faith brought a finger to her lips and pretended to ponder the name. "Is he a cousin?"

The girls burst into laughter.

"He's a dog," Hannah said.

"Big." Charlotte's arms went wide. "He slobbers when he kisses you."

Faith glanced at Ginny, who was gazing at her granddaughters with a soft look, then returned her attention to the twins. "Wow. Sounds like you had a wonderful night."

"We had chocolate chip pancakes this morning." Charlotte glanced at her twin and spoke quickly before Hannah could get it out. "And real juice from an orange."

"That Gramma squeezed herself." Hannah gestured to Ginny.

Out of the corner of her eye, Faith saw Graham gazing at the twins with pride, yes, but as if he were seeing them for the first time. Which made absolutely no sense.

"I take it you're here to make some candy." Faith glanced at Graham.

"If they'll be in the way…" Graham began.

"Don't be a worrywart," Ginny responded. "We talked about being safe around the stove. I'm going to show them how candy is made, then—"

"We get to eat some after," Hannah announced, her chest puffing out.

"Only the pieces Gramma is taking home." Charlotte tugged on Ginny's hand. "Right?"

"Correct." Ginny smiled and took each of the girl's hands. "The twins are mine until noon."

"We're always yours, Gramma." Hannah's comment prompted Ginny to pull both of her granddaughters close.

"That's right, you'll always be mine." When Ginny glanced at Graham, her eyes held a sheen. "You're on your own until noon."

She strode off in the direction of the kitchen with the twins skipping beside her.

Graham studied Faith, a smile hovering on his lips. "Where are you off to this morning?"

"How'd you know I was leaving?"

"The coat was my first clue." He flashed that smile, and she found herself wishing she didn't have to leave.

But, contrary to what her parents believed, her business wasn't a hobby where she "dabbled." Faith had clients and staff and obligations that had to be fulfilled.

"I'm heading into work." She inhaled the spicy scent of his cologne. It was subtle, but something about the smell and the man who wore it had her insides jiggling.

"Is your shop far?"

She smiled. "Nothing is far in Holly Pointe."

"I'd like to see it." He inclined his head. "Is now a good time?"

She hesitated only a fraction of a second, but it must have been long enough for him to notice.

"I can come by another time," he spoke hurriedly.

"No. I mean, you can certainly come another time if that works best for you. I'm happy to give you a quick tour. Then I'll need to get to work."

Faith wished she hadn't added that last little bit. She'd made it sound as if she thought he wanted to spend the day with her when he'd given no such indication.

"I understand the need to get something done, so I won't keep you long." He opened the door and made a sweeping gesture. "After you."

Faith stepped outside. When Graham took her arm, as naturally as if he'd been doing it for years, she smiled up at him. And when he returned her smile and his gaze dropped to her mouth, Faith felt the heat of the sun despite the cloudy sky.

# CHAPTER NINE

Graham didn't know what to think when Faith simply took off down the sidewalk in the direction of the business district. He assumed they'd drive to her shop. But, as she'd said, nothing was far in this town.

Everyone had scooped their walks, and there was some kind of salt on the surface. Although Graham needed to work on the project, and this was a prime time, considering Ginny had the twins, he found himself curious about what Faith actually did.

It was difficult to imagine how someone could make the transition from an NYC lifestyle to one in this rural Vermont town. Faith had not only done just that, all indications were that she was thriving here.

Graham saw the charm in this community where everyone was so friendly and kind. Still, he was surprised she'd been able to give up all the amenities of city life. And from everything she'd said, Faith had enjoyed a successful life in the city before relocating here.

"Santa is coming to the house this afternoon at four," Faith told him. "We set the date for when the elementary kids are out of school so that they can come. I don't know what you have on your schedule for this afternoon, but I think it'll be a highlight for the girls."

"Thanks for letting me know." Graham thought, though he couldn't be certain, that Tiffany took the twins every year to one of the stores in Manhattan to see Santa. It appeared this would be his year. "I'll make sure they see him. Though, didn't they already see him at the lake?"

The twins had spoken about seeing the reindeer, the sleigh and, of course, Santa all last weekend. Graham had loved hearing the excitement in their voices. He'd assumed, obviously in error, that the encounter had qualified as a visit with Santa.

"He spoke with the children, and they got to pet the reindeer," Faith acknowledged, slowing her pace as a row of buildings came into sight. "But when Santa comes to the Candy Cane Christmas House, it's an opportunity for the children to tell him what they want and for parents to snap some pictures."

"I'll definitely make sure they see him." Graham glanced around curiously as Faith pulled a huge brass key from her pocket and unlocked a door the color of mint.

*Faith Originals* was etched in a swirling font in the glass of the storefront. He stepped inside the warmth and took it all in.

There were signs everywhere with motivational sayings. Some were scrolled on weathered barn wood, others on glass or fabric. There were ones on small easels and others attached to photo clip string lights. The display tables and counters were arranged to not only show off the products, but to also exude a feeling of warmth.

"This is it." She swung her arm wide, encompassing the entire shop. "This is where I sell my wares. Here and on the internet. Online is actually where I do most of my business."

"Alone?"

"Pardon?"

"I can see how this would be a busy time of year for you. Surely you can't do this all yourself."

"No way." She motioned for him to follow her into the back. "This is where most of the work gets done."

"Hey, Faith."

"Hi, Faith."

The voices rang out from an assembly line of sorts where numerous women packaged items for shipping. In one corner of the large room, a woman sat in front of a computer. Taking off orders?

"Good morning, everyone." Faith placed a hand on Graham's shoulder. "This is a friend, Graham Westfall. He's visiting, and I thought I'd give him a tour."

This time, they called out his name in greeting. He noticed there was a good mix of ages in the room. While it was still early, he saw one of the women putting on her coat and waving good-bye.

Faith then took him into an empty room that looked more like a workshop, with paints, boards and ideas on a whiteboard.

"This is where you create," he murmured and was rewarded with a bright smile.

"When my parents visited, they said, 'So this is where you work.'" Her smile widened. "I like your observation much better."

"It's amazing." Graham had to admit he was impressed. Sure, this was on a small scale, and he wasn't into inspirational stuff, but he knew quality when he saw it. Faith not only had the talent, but she put out amazing products. "Why was the one woman leaving when the day is just getting started?"

Faith trailed her fingers along one counter. "As you can imagine, there isn't much opportunity for employment for women in a rural area. It's especially difficult for those who are caregivers, either for elderly parents or children."

"You help meet that need for employment."

"I do my best. Candy, she's the woman who left, has a mother she takes to radiation therapy in Burlington. She comes in early, then she'll return later to get in a few more hours."

"You unlocked the front door. Who's manning the showroom when you're back here with me?"

"You must not have noticed Sondra. She was the older woman with tight black curls who slipped out to the front when I arrived." Faith's expression softened. "She's my rock. Actually, everyone here is a big part of my success. I couldn't do this alone. Thanks to them, I don't have to."

Graham listened to her words, watched her face as she spoke about her employees, people who weren't just faceless names to her, and something inside him stirred. "You're a remarkable woman, Faith Pierson."

Her cheeks pinked, and she shook her head, a small smile lifting her lips. "I'm really quite ordinary."

Before he could analyze his actions, he stepped closer, cupping her cheek with his hand. "I'd say you're quite extraordinary."

Then his lips were on hers, and the spark that had been simmering between them ignited. He pulled her to him. Her arms went around his neck and she was kissing him back with a fervor that shattered his control.

When he swept his tongue over her lips, she emitted a little moan and opened to him. He probed the depths of her mouth with his tongue as his erection pressed against her belly.

If he'd been thinking, he would have realized that this was a place of business, and on the other side of the door were employees-her employees—who could walk in on them at any minute.

But any rational thought fled his brain as he moved his hand up to cup her breast, thankful she wore a cotton shirt today instead of a sweater. His thumb teased the tip of her nipple, and it went hard beneath his touch.

"Faith, I hope—"

The voice cut off.

It took a second for Graham to drop his hand and step back. Controlling his breathing took several more seconds.

Faith's eyes were bright and her lips swollen from his kisses as she turned to face Krista.

~

It was awkward, but no big deal. At least that's what Faith told herself as she and Graham greeted Krista and as Graham then made a hasty exit.

Now, she was left with Krista, whose eyes brimmed with curiosity.

"I'm glad I didn't bring the cameraman back with me." Krista's eyes danced. "He wanted to get some pictures of the assembly area and of the store."

"Cameraman?" Faith's voice might be steady, but her heart still beat an erratic rhythm, and certain parts of her anatomy burned for Graham's touch.

"We're filming the segment today for the show," Krista prompted. "Behind the scenes at Faith Originals."

"That's tomorrow."

Krista flashed a smile. "No. That's today."

"I must have put it on my calendar wrong." Faith nearly groaned aloud. How could she have made such a mistake? Last spring, Dustin and Krista had filmed a segment about her business. Sales had gone through the roof for a good three months.

What had touched her most was all the lovely comments she'd received on the business's Facebook page and her Instagram feed.

Krista had teased that Faith had been as much a hit as her business. That, Faith knew, was simply her friend being nice.

Since she'd already been featured, Faith was surprised that her friends wanted to spotlight her again, this time in early December, a prime time for the types of items she sold.

"I-I-" Faith stumbled over what to say. "I don't know what to say. How could something this important slip my mind?"

"Kisses have a way of doing that to you." Krista chuckled. "I swear that when Dustin kisses me, I don't know if I'm coming or going."

"I'm sorry about that—"

"Don't be sorry. Graham is a handsome man, and he seems quite nice. Why shouldn't you have some fun while he's in town?" Krista's voice turned matter-of-fact. "Not every relationship has to be a happily-ever-after, forever kind of thing. It's okay to be in the moment, too."

Put that way, it made sense.

"The man does know how to kiss," Faith murmured.

"I could see that." Krista grinned. "And based on the way he was blushing, you're no slouch yourself."

"Now, it's time for business." Faith glanced down at her shirt, skirt and boots. "This isn't what I planned to wear for the interview."

Krista stepped back and studied her. "Your outfit is fine. I brought along Angelique. The camera can be very unforgiving. She can touch up your makeup so it's camera-ready and make a few adjustments to your hair." Krista's mouth twitched with a barely contained smile. "It looks like someone's been running his hands through it."

Faith doubted Krista had ever looked anything but gorgeous in front of the camera, but she only nodded. From several things Krista had said, Faith knew the runway world was not the cushy life many thought.

Now, like her, Krista had found her niche. Her and Dustin's television show allowed them to work together and gave them more time to spend with their sons.

Dustin arrived just as Angelique pronounced Faith *beautiful* and *camera-ready*.

They filmed the interview in the shop, with Faith surrounded by items she'd designed. Dustin and Krista had an easy conversational style of interviewing, and Faith soon forgot they were being filmed. Talking with the couple was like, well, talking to friends.

"Okay, we've got what we need," Denny, the producer, announced and gave a thumbs-up.

"When will this segment air?" Knowing it was coming, Faith's "factory" had been stockpiling items in anticipation of large orders. Workers were also on alert, ready to put in increased hours.

"This Wednesday."

Faith widened her eyes. "That soon?"

Concern filled Dustin's gray eyes. "Will that be a problem? I can see if we can push the airing back."

"We just thought, for business reasons, you'd want the segment to be on sooner, rather than later," Krista added.

"No. Wednesday is wonderful." Faith took a deep breath, let it out. "I'll let my employees know. I want to thank you for doing this. Being on your show is a huge boost to my business."

"You being on our show is a huge ratings boost," Dustin said, his expression serious.

Faith chuckled. "That's nice of you to say."

"It's the truth." Dustin's gaze searched hers. "I don't believe you realize what a natural you are in front of the camera. Your products are top-notch and would likely sell themselves, but you add an authenticity to the sales."

"The public loves you, Faith. That kind of charisma is impossible to teach."

"You both are incredibly sweet." Faith gave them each a hug. "I'm blessed to have you in my life."

"Dustin and I have been talking…" Krista glanced at her husband and received his go-ahead nod. "We'd like to feature your products in our new store."

"Really?"

"Really," Dustin said. "That isn't all."

The excited gleam in their eyes had Faith dropping into the nearest chair. "I think I need to sit to hear the rest."

Dustin and Krista pulled up chairs and sat, facing her.

Faith wasn't sure what to think of their earnest expressions. "Tell me."

"Carrying your items in our store means you'll have to ramp up production. You can retain the small facility here in Holly Pointe, but it would be best if you took some of the factory space we've leased in Gatlinburg."

Faith blinked. "You really think that'd be necessary?"

"We do." Krista nodded. "Keeping the store here, along with limited output, would make your Holly Pointe operation a destination for tourists. Kind of like Ben & Jerry's in Waterbury. But the main production would happen in Tennessee."

"You'd be able to simply create, and there would be people to follow through on your designs and ideas." Dustin's voice turned persuasive. "You'd have the time to do what you do best...and we hope time for one other enterprise."

Faith inclined her head.

"We'd like you to be one of the voices of our brand." Dustin held up a hand when Faith opened her mouth, as if he sensed the words of refusal pushing against her lips. "Hear me out. There's something about you that speaks to warmth and trust and down-home goodness. Our audience responded very positively to you."

"I'm not trained—"

"Neither Dustin nor I were trained to run a television show, but we learned." Krista put a hand on Faith's arm and leaned forward. "I realize this is a big decision. Think about it. Come up with your questions, and we'll discuss it again."

Faith opened her mouth, then shut it. She knew plenty of people who would kill for this opportunity. While she didn't believe she was one of those, past experience had taught her the value of thinking through major decisions. "Thank you. I'll definitely think about it."

As if by tacit agreement, the two stood.

"Krista and I are taking the boys out to Landers Tree Farm

tomorrow morning." Dustin glanced at Krista. "Do you know if Graham is putting up a tree?"

Faith smiled, happy that the discussion had veered off the business track. "He doesn't have one yet, but I know he promised the twins he'd be getting them one."

"We'd like to get to know him better, since we may be working with him on the ad campaign." Krista pushed back a lock of silky hair. "We were thinking of going to Landers at ten. Maybe you could see if he'd be interested in bringing the girls and coming with us?"

Faith had no doubts the outing was something Graham would make time for. "I'll ask. Or I can give you his number, and you can call him direct? That might be better than me being in the middle."

"Sounds like a pl—" Dustin began.

Krista put a staying hand on her husband's arm, her smiling gaze remaining focused on Faith. "Why don't you just ask Graham? And plan to come along, too."

# CHAPTER TEN

Graham's thoughts were still spinning by the time he arrived back at the Candy Cane Christmas House. He couldn't believe he'd lost control when he'd kissed Faith. He never lost control.

There was something about Faith...

"Come back for the cookie baking," Mary called out to the group of women leaving with containers of what Graham assumed was candy. "Next Friday."

A chorus of "I'll be there" and "Wouldn't miss it" filled the air.

Graham stepped aside on the porch and found himself the recipient of smiles and greetings. He swore he'd been greeted and smiled at more since he'd arrived in Holly Pointe than he had in the entire last year.

The second he stepped into the house, the scent of chocolate and sugar had him taking a deep breath. He realized he was still off-balanced from the incident with Faith. Now that he'd had a little time—okay, not all that much time, but enough, as well as some distance—he wondered what he'd been thinking.

He liked her. That was a given. Another given was they lived in two very different worlds. He was happy in his. She was extremely happy in hers.

He also wanted her. In a way he couldn't recall wanting any woman since Steph had died.

A brief liaison?

The notion that marriage had to follow a sexual relationship was archaic and outdated. But for all her quirkiness, Faith seemed more of a traditionalist.

"Graham." Ginny crossed the room to him.

He glanced around, expecting to see his girls following in her wake, but didn't see them. "Where are the girls?"

"Upstairs napping."

"Seriously?" Graham didn't recall exactly when, but he definitely recalled Tiffany telling him around age three—or maybe it was four—that the twins had given up their nap.

Since the change hadn't impacted him, he hadn't paid the news much mind.

"I think last night wore them out," Ginny admitted with a wry smile. "They were up later than usual. And even though they thought sleeping on the air mattresses was a great adventure, I'm not sure they slept well."

"They just said they wanted to take a nap?" Somehow, Graham couldn't see either girl suggesting that option. Not with so much activity going on in the house.

Ginny laughed as if she found the idea as unbelievable as he did. "Oh my goodness, no. They were picking at each other, so I suggested we go upstairs so they could play with their ponies. The quiet play appeared to relax them. I suggested they lie on their beds and I'd read to them. They both were asleep by the middle of book three."

Graham stared at his mother-in-law in amazement. "You're a wonder."

Pleasure suffused her lined face. "I'm just a grandma."

"I'm glad they've had this chance to get to know you better."

"Not as glad as I am." Ginny smiled. "I need to get home to

make dinner for the descending herd, but I was wondering if you have time to share a quick cup of cocoa with me."

Actually, Graham really needed to get some work done, but he knew he wouldn't be very productive with all these thoughts of Faith swirling in his head. Maybe a cup of cocoa would help him settle. "I'd like that."

At that moment, a burst of laughter sounded from the kitchen. He smiled. "I don't think we're going to be able to hear ourselves in there."

"I checked your cupboards and the refrigerator upstairs. You have what I need to make cocoa."

"In that case," Graham swept an arm, "lead the way."

Ten minutes later, they were seated in the small kitchen, cups of steaming peppermint hot chocolate, complete with a candy cane stick, in front of them.

"I want to tell you again how sorry I am that I didn't have room for you to—"

"Ginny. It's okay. Really."

"I feel partly to blame."

"I don't understand how."

"I let Shawn know at Thanksgiving that I'd bought the family lift tickets to Jay Peak for Christmas. They're expensive, but I know money is tight. I thought they'd come after the holidays." Ginny stirred her cocoa with the candy stick. "Shawn has always been impulsive, but I never thought he'd pack everyone in the car and drive here."

"It's good he did." Graham reached across the table and covered her free hand with his. "Family is what this time of year is all about."

Then why, Graham wondered, had he spent the past couple of Christmases in New York with no family? His parents, well, they had their own new families. But Ginny. Why had he not reached out?

"Steph has been gone almost three years, Graham."

He looked up, met her direct gaze.

"She would want you to be happy," she said. "To find someone who makes you happy."

"I don't have time to find that someone," he told Ginny honestly, not wanting to get into what Steph would want or not want for him. He'd let her down. The day she died, he'd let her down big-time. Based on how he'd behaved, he wasn't sure he deserved another shot at happiness. Even if he'd had the time. "My job is a time suck, and the girls, well, even with a nanny, they take time."

"You're a young man. You shouldn't have to go through your life alone."

Graham stared at this woman who'd been kind to him from the first time Steph had brought him home. Ginny was the one who'd comforted him after the accident. The one who had stayed with him and the girls until he'd gotten himself together. All that, while dealing with her own profound grief.

"You hear all the jokes about mothers-in-law." Graham leaned forward, his gaze on her face. "But I hit the jackpot. I'm lucky to have you in my life. The twins are lucky to have you as their grandma."

Tears sprang to Ginny's eyes. "I believe that's the nicest thing anyone has ever said to me."

"I should have done more to get you and the girls together, made more of an effort." Graham blew out a breath and decided complete honesty was in order. Especially with Ginny staring at him as if he'd hung the moon. "I only came here this year because I gave Tiffany the month off and needed someone to watch the twins."

He expected Ginny to look shocked, then disapproving, but her smile didn't waver as she brought the cup to her lips and took a long sip. "I know life for you hasn't been easy. I wanted to help. Which is why I feel—"

Holding up a hand to stop her, Graham shook his head. "This

is officially an apology-free zone. I don't want to hear any more apologies from you."

"And I don't want to hear any more apologies from you." Ginny set down her cup and pointed a finger at him. "Agreed?"

"Agreed."

"Now, tell me about the party." Ginny fixed those clear blue eyes on him. "There wasn't really time earlier. It sounded as if you and Faith had fun?"

"We did. The drive up was a little interesting, but the house and..." Graham found himself telling her details he hadn't realized he'd noticed. The way everyone seemed to know and like Faith. How kind she was to everyone. "Even though on the surface she's as different from Steph as she could possibly be, there's something about her..."

Graham stopped himself before he could tell her about kissing Faith and how he wanted her so badly he ached. Sexual attraction was an off-limits topic with a former mother-in-law. Or if it wasn't, it should be.

Ginny nodded. "Faith is different than Steph in many ways, but they both have good hearts."

Graham nodded. He drank his cocoa and resisted the urge to say more, fearing if he did it might be something he'd regret.

"It's difficult being a single woman in a small town." Ginny appeared to ponder her next words. "There aren't many men for women to choose from. I suppose it's the same for single men. You're lucky if you find that special someone here."

"Faith has a lot going for her."

Ginny nodded. "She does. She's smart and kind and caring. She's also an excellent businesswoman and good to her employees. Mary grew to depend on her, but I told Mary today that she's capable of doing so much more."

"Mary is? Really?"

Ginny hesitated for only a moment. "Mary has a great many friends here, but no family. When she got sick, Faith came. She filled a void in Mary's life. There isn't a single doubt in my mind that for those first six months, Mary needed Faith's comfort and support. Now it's time for Mary to let Faith know she's healed."

"You think Mary is afraid if Faith discovers she doesn't need her, that she'll leave?"

"I do. I don't know whether Faith will or not. I think Faith genuinely loves it here. But we should never make such important decisions for other people. Mary needs to let Faith decide." Ginny's expression turned introspective. "I know how difficult that can be."

Graham cocked his head.

"I didn't want my girl striking out on her own, going to that big city to pursue her dreams. That's what she wanted, and I had to let her go." Ginny's lips curved. "It all worked out."

Something inside Graham went cold. "How can you say that?" His voice was taut with barely restrained control. "Steph is dead."

Ginny didn't immediately respond. When she set her cup down with slow, controlled movements, the eyes that met his were firm and direct. "Steph had friends who supported and encouraged her. She had a career she loved. Then she met you and fell in love. She got married and gave birth to two healthy girls. Sounds to me like a life well-lived."

"She was too young to die." The bleakness of the words threatened to overtake him.

"You won't get any disagreement from me on that score." A sadness stole over Ginny's features. "When you've lived as long as I have, you'll see many friends and family leave this earth far too early."

"If I'd stayed home, instead of leaving on that trip, I could have taken Charlotte to the doctor. Steph could have stayed home with Hannah."

"Then it may have been you who died, instead of my girl."

"How can you not hate me for that? For not being there for Steph when she needed me."

Though they'd had many conversations, in the aftermath of Steph's death and in the years that followed, his whereabouts that night had never been discussed.

"The meeting in Chicago was a good opportunity," he began. "That was the truth. But I could have gotten out of it. I thought I needed a break from my home life, and I took it. Steph paid the price. If she'd been at home—"

"Graham," Ginny interrupted. "There's an old saying. If the good Lord wants you, he'll find you hiding under the bed."

"I don't want anything to do with a God who'd take a woman as young and vibrant as Steph, someone with two little girls who needed her." Graham's voice had begun to crack, and he bore down hard. "I needed her. The girls needed her."

"Life isn't fair. What happened to my Stephanie wasn't fair." Ginny's eyes filled with sympathy. "You need to let the guilt you feel go. For your sake and for your daughters' sake as well."

"I know." Graham raked a hand through his hair. "It's just this thing with Faith has me all discombobulated."

"The attraction, you mean." Ginny's blue eyes, which had been cloudy only a second before, twinkled. "I think you should pursue it."

Graham choked on his cocoa. He set the cup down, unable to believe what he was hearing. "Really? Even though I'll be heading back to the city at the end of the month?"

"None of us knows what the future holds. The way I look at it, as long as you're both going into this...well, whatever you want to call it, with your eyes wide open, why not enjoy each other and your time together?"

Pushing back her chair, Ginny rose. "I need to get back and prepare dinner. I can't believe how much my grandsons eat. No wonder Shawn and Morgan are always short of cash." Ginny laughed. "If I had to feed those boys every day, my wallet would be empty, too."

After making sure the girls were still sleeping, Graham walked Ginny to the front door and helped her on with her coat.

Then, impulsively, he pulled her in for a hug. "Thank you," he whispered against her hair. "You're the best."

She returned the hug, then stepped back. "Anytime you want to talk, know I'm here for you. I love you, Graham."

He watched her walk out the door and stood staring into the falling snow until she disappeared from view. Then he went back upstairs, determined to work until his daughters woke up.

Faith's head was still spinning when she arrived home at seven, in desperate need of food and a few minutes of quiet. The second she stepped inside the house, she realized if food and quiet were what she craved, she should have stopped at Rosie's Diner and sat in a corner booth far from the hubbub.

She'd forgotten that tonight was a gift-wrapping marathon. Several people in the community who had stellar wrapping skills had volunteered to help and instruct others on wrapping gifts. Some were there to wrap gifts for the troops and for those in the community who were homebound or lived in nursing homes.

The night was always a raucous event, with wine—sparkling punch for those who didn't drink—lots of ribbon and paper and laughter. At the end of the evening, they played games in which participants could win plates of cookies and fudge to take home.

Normally, Faith loved being involved. In the past couple of years, she'd had to be involved because Mary simply hadn't felt up to it. Instead, her grandmother had sat in her favorite rocking chair and watched the activities while Faith took charge.

Guilt flooded Faith. She should have been home thirty minutes ago to help get everything organized so she could be at the door when guests began arriving for the seven o'clock start time.

To her surprise, it appeared everything was running smoothly, with her grandmother directing activities at the different stations.

Faith blinked as if seeing a ghost. This was the grandmother she remembered. Take-charge Mary, a master at organization, a dynamo who had only one speed—fast. Seeing her now, it would be easy to believe the last three years had been a bad dream.

She was still staring, watching Mel show a woman Faith recognized from church how to tie an intricate bow when Mary noticed her and crossed the room.

"You've got everything under control," Faith blurted.

Mary's eyes twinkled, actually twinkled. "Don't sound so surprised. I've run a few of these wrapping parties in my day."

"What can I do to help?"

Her grandmother studied her. "I wager you haven't eaten dinner yet."

Faith waved a dismissive hand. "I had a big lunch. I'm fine."

"Go in and make yourself a sandwich." Mary patted her shoulder. "Put your feet up. Everything is under control here."

"Are you sure?"

Mary gestured with one hand toward the buzzing parlor. "Doesn't it look under control?"

"It does."

"Relax. Have a cup of tea. Or maybe a glass of wine." Mary smiled. "I'm enjoying myself immensely, Faith. Overseeing this is giving me pleasure."

A kind way of saying, *Let me have this moment*. Faith was happy to oblige.

"If you need an extra pair of hands for anything, you know where to find me."

"I won't, but thank you." Mary brushed a kiss, whisper soft, against Faith's cheek. "You look tired and a bit stressed. Take some time to unwind."

Faith waved to her friends, who were too busy to do anything but smile back, then stepped into the quiet of the large kitchen.

She made herself a sandwich with roast beef and two slices of homemade oat bread. Instead of tea—or wine—she opted for a cold glass of milk. Then she did as her grandmother had instructed and put her feet up.

The last bite of the delicious sandwich had barely disappeared when Graham ambled into the kitchen. He stopped short at the sight of her.

"Faith." A smile lit up his face. "I didn't know you were home."

She dropped her feet from the chair and straightened, pleasure rippling through her at the sight of him. Wearing jeans and a ski sweater, he was dressed even more casually than when she'd seen him earlier.

If he'd shaved today, it didn't show, and a dusting of dark scruff covered his cheeks. His hair, instead of falling into perfect place, looked as if he'd just ran his hands through it.

The urge to stand and run her fingers through it and brush her knuckles against that scruff teased and tempted. She settled for a smile. "Care to join me?"

In answer, he dropped down into the chair opposite her. "You're just now eating?"

He gestured to the plate with only a few crumbs remaining.

"I got caught up working and lost track of time." Her lips tipped in a rueful smile. "I even forgot tonight was gift-wrapping."

"Your grandmother reminds me of a general marshaling the troops."

"I noticed that." She shook her head. "It's like a miracle. I don't know how or why the turnaround, but I'm thrilled."

She realized suddenly that her pleasure over seeing her grandmother so vibrant had shoved aside thoughts of Krista's business proposition. Not to mention her growing feelings for Graham.

Now, those thoughts flooded back.

"—the girls."

Faith blinked. "Where are the girls?"

"Did you tune me out, Ms. Pierson?"

His teasing tone had heat burning her cheeks.

"It was a just a business thing that—" She waved a dismissive hand. "Where are the twins?"

"Where do you think?" He gave a little laugh, gestured with his head in the direction of the other room. "They took a nap this afternoon. Now they're firing on all cylinders. At the moment, they're on ribbon and wrapping paper duty. Anyone who needs a certain color of ribbon or a specific roll of paper asks them, and they get it. They are taking their jobs quite seriously."

"I'm glad they're having fun." Faith paused. "On the way home, I thought about seeing if they'd be interested in building a snowman in the backyard. While the front is more for the community, I usually try to build one for myself every year."

Faith flushed. Only after the words had left her lips did she realize how they sounded. A thirty-year-old woman who built a snowman for herself every year?

"I think they'd love it. I know I would." Graham shot her a conspiratorial smile. "When I was a little boy, I always wanted to build a snowman. But my father, when we were in the house in Connecticut, considered them eyesores. Until they helped with the massive one in your front yard, the girls had never had the experience. That's on me."

He took a lot on himself, Faith realized. Typical, she thought, of a high-achieving personality. She recognized it because her family was made up of type A, high achievers.

"Which reminds me, I still need to get a tree. I promised them we'd get and decorate one this year, and I've yet to follow through on that."

Faith thought of Krista's offer and decided, after the snowman, they could discuss getting a tree.

# CHAPTER ELEVEN

Graham didn't know if it was the nap or the excitement that made building the snowman in the backyard so much fun.

"Lift me so I can give him his eyes," Charlotte said, then paused to add, "Please."

"I've got the carrot for the nose." Hannah held it out in case he'd missed Faith handing it to her only seconds before.

"Your dad and I will do the mouth," Faith added, taking it upon herself to lift Hannah so she could stick in the nose right after Charlotte finished with the eyes.

Faith gave a handful of pebbles to Graham, and they carefully formed the mouth.

"Now, let's step back and say hello to our snowman."

Hands on hips, Faith surveyed the snowman, who stood nearly as tall as Graham.

Graham had sacrificed the scarf he'd been wearing to drape it around the snowman. He had to admit the bright blue cashmere gave the snowman a jaunty air.

Charlotte clapped her hands.

"Be-u-ti-ful," Hannah declared.

"You know, there's a tradition after you finish building a snowman," Faith said.

Graham cocked his head, unsure where she was going with this. He'd never heard of any tradition. Then again, he was hardly the expert when it came to such activities.

"Snowball fight." With those words, Faith scooped up a handful of the white stuff, and a second later, a snowball hit Graham in the chest.

The twins dissolved in giggles, while he lightly packed snow in each hand and tossed it at them.

The fight was on, and it lasted until they were all cold, wet and red-faced with laughter.

Tromping into the back-porch area, or what Mary referred to as the mudroom, they peeled off boots and socks and gloves, hung coats on wall pegs and doffed hats crusted with snow.

"It's been fun—" Faith began, but Graham cut her off by taking her hand.

"Do you need to help with the wrapping?"

She shook her hand, her ice-cold fingers curving around his. "It's wrapping up." She grinned at her pun. "I couldn't resist."

"Why don't you come upstairs? The girls will take showers and head to bed. I'll make you something hot to drink, and we can catch up on each other's day."

Graham's tone was light, but his eyes lingered on her lips. When he realized what was happening, he pulled his gaze to her eyes and saw the twinkle.

"Sounds like a good idea. Give me a few minutes. I'm going to make sure Mary doesn't need me, then change into something more comfortable."

He grinned at her words, and she returned the smile before he shifted his focus to his daughters. "Is there anything you want to tell Faith?"

The twins exchanged puzzled glances.

"Thank you for letting us use your snow," Hannah said promptly.

"Thank you for not hitting me in the face with a snowball," Charlotte said with an almost-prim smile.

Faith chuckled. "Thank you for making this evening so much fun."

As Graham ushered the girls up the stairs and listened to their excited chatter while they relived every moment of the snowman-building and the snowball fight, he realized Faith had summed up the evening perfectly.

*Fun.* It had been a fun evening.

How long had it been since he and his daughters had done something so enjoyable together? Oh, he'd taken them to FAO Schwarz shopping or walked the High Line a couple of times, but romping in a backyard in a boatload of snow...no, this evening definitely topped them all.

As they reached the second floor, Graham decided it was time to carry through on another promise. "You know what we're going to do tomorrow?"

"Another snowball fight?" Charlotte asked hopefully.

"Even better," he said. "Tomorrow, we're going to get a Christmas tree and decorate it."

When they hugged him, letting out little squeals, his heart swelled with emotion. He wasn't sure where he'd find this tree or where they'd get decorations, but he'd make it happen.

For their sakes. And, he realized, for his own.

A small part of Faith wished Mary had needed her help. But by the time she changed out of her wet clothes and into flannel pants and a soft tee, everyone had gone.

Faith thought there might be cleanup left, but the parlor had been set to rights and was ready for tomorrow's activity,

Christmas bingo. It was Mary's favorite event of the season, with Santa—Kenny—acting as the bingo caller.

When she told Mary she was going upstairs to have a cup of something hot with Graham, her grandmother had only patted her arm and told her to have a good evening. Mary made it clear she was heading to bed and didn't want to be disturbed.

Faith had the vague feeling she'd been given free rein to do whatever she wanted. Like bringing a boy home to a house where no parents were in residence.

What a silly thought, she told herself as she knocked lightly on Graham's door at the top of the steps.

"Come in," he called out.

When Faith turned the knob, she found the door unlocked.

"We're back here."

She followed the sound to the back bedroom, which was where the twins slept. The girls were still awake. For now, anyway.

Huddled close in a double bed in nightgowns covered in sheep, they smiled as she stepped into the room.

"Daddy is reading us stories," Charlotte announced, as if that wasn't clear by the fact that Graham held an open book in his hands while he sat on the edge of the bed.

"We're on the second book. I picked the first," Hannah said. "Charlotte picked the second. We thought maybe we'd let Daddy pick the third."

"Faith should pick the third." Charlotte gave a decisive nod. "Daddy picked the third last night."

Hannah cocked her head, considered, then nodded. "Yes. You pick the third."

When Graham patted the spot on the bed beside him, Faith saw no other option but to sit there. There wasn't room for a chair in this smaller bedroom, so her choices were limited to standing or sitting on the bed.

"I don't know what kind of books you like," Faith said.

"They brought only their favorites," Graham informed her. "You can't go wrong picking any of them."

He'd shaved and showered since the snowball fight, his hair still damp at the ends and curling just a little. He smelled wonderful, and if it wouldn't have looked ridiculous, she might have opted for self-preservation and headed for the far end of the bed.

"Okay." She spoke easily, her tone giving no indication of her galloping heartbeat. "Once you're done with this book, I'll pick the third."

The girls only smiled as if they hadn't a single doubt that's what would happen.

The book he was reading was about two hedgehogs.

Faith had to smile as Graham read the character voices. He mixed them up with Hattie having a high, almost-falsetto quality, while Horace sounded like a cross between Louis Armstrong and James Earl Jones.

The twins paid rapt attention and smiled at the end when Horace and Hattie realized that everyone was wonderful in their own way.

The girls' eyelids had begun to droop, but if she'd thought she could pass on reading the third, she was mistaken. Their gazes shifted to her as soon as Graham closed the book, telling her that wasn't happening.

"What books do I have to choose from?" Faith asked, glancing around the room.

Graham pointed to a tall stack of books atop the small dresser. "Any of those. The smaller bunch are ones we've read since coming to Holly Pointe."

Faith glanced through the stack, then saw one that appeared to have the same characters as the one Graham had just read. She was intrigued by Horace and Hattie. Besides, she loved books in a series, and she bet the twins did, too.

"What about this one?" She held it up, showing the twins the cover.

"Yay." Charlotte glanced at her sister. "I knew she'd pick a good one."

If Graham was to be believed, these all fell into the category of "good ones."

She ran into trouble almost immediately as she tried to mimic Graham's skill at voices. Charlotte's lips twitched first at Faith's attempt to reach the depths of Horace's voice.

"You sound like a frog." Charlotte giggled.

"Charlotte." Graham fixed his gaze on Charlotte, and her smile vanished. "Is that kind?"

"No." Charlotte's lips drooped like a chastened clown's. "I'm sorry."

"I've got an idea. What if your dad reads Horace's voice, and I read Hattie's?"

"Yes," Hannah said immediately. "Do that."

Charlotte nodded vigorously.

Sharing the book meant moving even closer to Graham. His fingers brushed hers as he reached out to help her hold it.

The sizzle had her bobbling her side of the book, and his eyes were hot on hers when they met. Faith had to clear her throat before she began. But after that rocky start, the story progressed smoothly. By the time she reached the end, Faith was eager to know more about the adventures of the hedgehogs and their friends.

"That's all for tonight." Graham shut the book, then turned to her. "Thank you, Faith."

She watched him kiss each girl's forehead and tuck the covers up around them. An action that had to be redone after the girls bolted upright to give Faith hugs.

Her heart felt ten times its normal size as she and Graham slipped from the room, making sure the night-light was on.

He closed the door behind them and shot her a wicked grin that had her heart lurching. "Now it's time to party."

"Par-ty?" She choked out the word.

"Tell me what you'd like to drink. I have Earl Grey and Earl Grey."

Faith laughed and brought a finger to her lips. "Why, I think I'll have the Earl Grey."

Graham and Faith worked together in the small kitchen. Not only did he have the tea, but he also had peppermint bark from the candy-making extravaganza.

He took a seat on the sofa in the tiny living space. Instead of sitting beside him, Faith commandeered a chair that was stylish but uncomfortable.

"Thanks for being a good sport about reading the story." He took a sip of the tea. "I didn't mean to put you on the spot."

"You didn't, and I enjoyed it." She bit into the delicious bark.

As she chewed, Graham noticed several bits of peppermint crumbs remained on her lips. He wondered what she'd think if he leaned forward and kissed them away.

Unfortunately, she blotted her mouth with a paper napkin festooned with frolicking Santas, and the crumbs were history.

"How did your day go?" he asked, realizing that he'd hardly seen her at all today.

"It went well. Krista and Dustin came to the shop with their production crew to film a segment for their show."

Graham's fingers, holding a jagged piece of bark, paused halfway to his mouth. "I thought you'd already been featured on their show."

She washed the bark down with a swig of tea. "I guess you could say I was so popular the first time, they demanded a repeat performance."

"That's wonderful."

"It is and it isn't." Her expression turned pensive.

He waited for her to say more. When she didn't, he went for levity. "Are you concerned about filling all the millions of orders coming your way?"

She smiled at the gross exaggeration. "This taping has been in the works for a while, so we're prepared for the increase in orders. I wasn't prepared for their offer."

"What kind of offer?"

Two lines formed between her brows. "They want to carry my items in their new store in Gatlinburg."

"Faith, that's wonderful! Congratulations."

"It is." She took a sip of tea, and her saucer jiggled so much she set it down.

Wanting to soothe her, he captured her hand and found it ice-cold. "What's the matter?"

"They want to go big with my products. They offered to let me use factory space in Tennessee for the production of my designs. Dustin and Krista seem certain that will be necessary."

Graham tugged her over to the sofa to sit beside him. "What about your shop here and the people you employ?"

"They said it'd be good to keep it and that it will help Holly Pointe become a destination for those who love my products… kind of like Ben & Jerry's in Waterbury, only without the yummy ice cream."

He chuckled, then immediately sobered. "You don't appear sold on the idea."

She blew out a breath. "They also want me to be a regular on their show. Apparently, the viewing public reacts well to me."

Graham nodded. "I can see that."

"I'm just not sure going big is what I want." She leaned her head back against the sofa. "Until I saw Mary tonight, in her element and back to how she used to be before the pneumonia knocked her back, I was thinking there's no way I could leave her."

"Then you saw her, and that excuse went out the window."

"Exactly."

"Which is good."

Her brows furrowed as she shifted to face him.

"Think about it. You'd have used her as an excuse instead of considering what you really want to do. This way, whatever you decide, it will be your choice." Graham tightened his fingers around hers. "There are lots of reasons to stay. And lots of reasons to seize this opportunity."

"What do you think I should do?" When he started to shake his head, she continued without giving him a chance to speak. "I'm not asking you to make the decision for me. I'm simply asking for your opinion."

"I can honestly see the advantages of both." The choice, for him, would be clear. Dustin and Krista were offering Faith a once-in-a-lifetime opportunity. But his goals and Faith's weren't aligned. "If I were you, I'd make a pro-con list and discuss your options with people you trust. See if the list and what others say help bring clarity."

"I trust you," she told him, her voice turning husky as she leaned close. "That's why I asked."

"I'm flattered." Graham wanted to kiss her. Instead, he released her hand and abruptly stood. "I'll be right back."

# CHAPTER TWELVE

Faith stared at Graham's back and tried to make sense of what had just happened. He'd been ready to kiss her. She'd been absolutely—okay, *nearly*—sure of that when he'd surged to his feet like a scalded cat.

She'd been ready to slink down the stairs when he'd turned back and flashed her a smile that had her heart pitter-pattering.

In a matter of seconds, he was back and sitting beside her, his arm around her.

"Why did you leave?"

He flashed a rueful smile. "I remembered the two little girls just down the hall. Once they're asleep, they're down for the count. But sometimes they lie there and talk, then get up and want a drink of water. I wanted to make sure we wouldn't have to worry about being disturbed."

The pitter-patter became a salsa rhythm. "You don't want them to overhear our conversation?"

He trailed a finger down her face. "Not conversation, but this."

His mouth closed over hers, and every fiber of her being

broke into the *Hallelujah Chorus*. It was as if she was starved and hadn't realized it until this moment.

The kiss might have started out sweet, but the underlying fire set her insides to blazing. She pressed herself against him, not able to get close enough.

His tongue swept her lips, and her mouth opened to his probing tongue. It was as if he was inside her already, and she wanted him there with a desperation she'd never felt.

They kissed like that for the longest time. When his hand slipped under her shirt to unclasp her bra, she wanted to weep with relief. His fingers, ah, those magic fingers soon had her breasts aching with need. She wanted his mouth on her. Needed his mouth on her.

But when he pushed up the hem of her shirt, she shook her head. "Not out here."

Her voice, raspy and raw with need, captured his attention.

"Your bedroom. There's a lock."

Regardless of what he'd said about the twins being sound sleepers, Faith wasn't going to risk them seeing something they shouldn't see.

"Let's go." He took her hand, and they stumbled against each other in the tiny hallway, stifling their laughter.

Only when the door was firmly locked did Faith remember there was one other thing. "Condoms? I'm not on the pill."

The blank look on his face for that single second had her heart plummeting.

Then his expression cleared. "Give me a moment."

He rummaged through his dresser drawer and pulled out several foil packets.

"Are they still good?" Faith lifted the packets from his fingers and read the date on the foil wrapper. "Looks like we're covered."

Brushing her hair back from her face, he kissed her on the mouth with such intensity Faith's knees went weak. She found herself clinging to him as need and desire merged to become an inferno.

Stepping back, she pulled the shirt over her head and tossed the unclasped bra off to the side. "Now that's out of the way."

He stared at her breasts with their peach-colored nipples and taut tips. "You take my breath away."

She crooked her finger. "What are you doing way over there? And why do you have so many clothes on?"

Before long, his clothes were on the floor next to hers, and they were on the bed.

He talked while he made love to her, whispering sweet things as his hands explored her body, as his mouth followed in its wake.

Stroking, caressing and kissing her until every nerve ending vibrated with need for him.

"I want you," she whispered against his ear. "Inside me."

After slipping on the condom, he gave her what she wanted—what was obvious he wanted, too—but as he slid inside her, he continued to make love to her with his hands and his mouth as their bodies fell into a rhythm as old as time.

Faith hadn't had many lovers. Only three, and that counted her almost-fiancé, Thomas. But these feelings, this intense yearning and need, were something she'd never experienced before.

"I don't want this to end," she moaned as the orgasm began to ripple through her. "But I can't stop it."

"Let go." He took her earlobe between his teeth, and Faith lost control.

She clamped her legs around him, her nails digging into his shoulders as she went over the crest. Still, he continued to pump, as if determined to wring every last ounce of pleasure from her.

When she sagged against him, he took his own release, surging and calling out her name before collapsing on her.

Faith's heart hammered while everything inside her relaxed.

She wasn't sure where she found the energy to wrap her arms around him, but she did, planting a kiss against his neck.

She couldn't recall ever feeling this warm, this comfortable, this...satisfied.

His arm tightened around her, and he kissed her hair. "That was amazing."

She smiled against his muscular chest. "It was."

"Sometimes, when something is so good, you shouldn't even attempt to top it."

Faith could see where he was going with this. "I like the way you think."

He chuckled, and she felt him grow hard again within her. Within seconds, she was on top of him and gazing down into his glittering eyes. "Then you're really going to like this."

Faith left Graham's bed sometime during the night. After round two of making love, they'd both slept, with her cuddled up beside him, her soft brown hair a tantalizing cloud against his chest.

She smelled like vanilla, a scent that made him think of everything sweet. But as sweet as she was, she had a wild side to her in bed that he liked very much. He could tell the first time that they made love that she was unsure how much to give back. The second time, she'd given as good as she got.

His pillow still smelled of her. Graham inhaled deeply. Just the scent and the memory of her body under him had him hardening.

A cold shower took care of that issue, and by the time he was dressed and the bed was made, the twins were beginning to stir. On the way to their room, he checked his phone and found a text from Faith.

*Forgot to mention. Krista & Dustin asked if you, the girls and me would like to go look for a tree with them. Interested?*

Graham had to smile. Unlike most of those he corresponded with via text, Faith appeared to prefer complete sentences and spelling everything out.

Just one more thing to like about her.

He thought about his plans for the day, which involved working on the proposal and keeping the twins occupied.

The essence of Dustin and Krista's brand still hadn't solidified in his head. That was standing in the way of him nailing this new ad campaign. Spending time with them would give him the opportunity to know them better.

Know me, know my brand?

*Sure,* he texted back. *Time?*

*Ten o'clock,* came her reply. *We could meet downstairs at 9:45??*

He replied with a thumbs-up and turned to find his daughters, sleepy-eyed and hungry, watching him. "Guess what we're doing today?"

Graham didn't know the first thing about picking out a Christmas tree. Oh, he knew that he liked his trees full with a good shape, but other than that, he let the people who brought the tree to his apartment and set it up handle the pesky details.

Now, he stood with Faith and the twins in a field of trees that stretched in all directions on the rolling hillside. Dustin and Krista, in search of a taller tree for their great room, had wandered farther up the hill with their sons.

"We don't want anything too big." Graham rubbed his chin, speaking almost to himself. "The living room is small, and I still need room to work."

When Charlotte pointed to a tree that had to be seven feet tall, he shook his head and watched her smile turn to a frown.

"I like it," she said, her voice just shy of a whine.

"Think of this like we're detectives and this is a puzzle we have to solve." Faith, looking pretty as ever in her puffy coat and hat with plaid earflaps, put her hands on her hips. "One of the clues is we need to find a tree no taller than me."

"Maybe one with a nice shape." Graham made the shape he was looking for with his hands.

"One with soft bristles," Hannah said, getting into the game.

Graham thought about correcting her, but didn't want to dampen her enthusiasm.

Charlotte brought a finger to her lips, a thoughtful expression on her face. "It needs to have a stem at the top where we can put a star...or an angel."

"Good puzzle pieces," Faith said before Graham could respond. "Now the search begins."

The twins raced off. It felt natural to take Faith's arm as they trudged through the snow.

"I enjoyed last night." Though no one was nearby, he kept his voice low.

"I did, too."

Graham wasn't sure if the flush on her cheeks was from the cool breeze or because of the night they'd spent together. He hoped it had to do with pleasant memories of the two of them together.

"It's beautiful out here." She inhaled deeply, and a look of serenity crossed her face.

"It is." But his eyes weren't on the rolling hills of white dotted with tall trees of green, but on her. He took a step closer, his eyes on her mouth.

She lifted her face, and the sunlight streaming from the bright blue sky bathed her face in light.

"I found it." Charlotte's voice rang out.

"*We* found it." Hannah's voice rang out a second later.

Expelling a resigned breath, Graham took Faith's arm and headed for what he hoped was the perfect tree.

A half hour later, with the tree safely secured to the top of

Faith's Subaru and Dustin and Krista's tree on the schedule to be delivered later that afternoon, the couple and their children stood near the bottom of a nearby hill.

"Please, Daddy, please," one of their boys pleaded. "We want to sled."

"You promised," the other one said.

"Sled?" Graham asked.

Dustin gestured to a hill off to their right. "The Landers, who own this tree farm, make the slope available to anyone who buys a tree."

"There are any number of good sledding spots in the area, but the boys love this particular one," Krista added.

"I wish I'd have known," Graham said when he saw his girls' eyes light up. He shrugged. "But we didn't bring sleds."

"You don't have to." Faith jumped into the conversation and gestured to a small wooden building not far from them. "There are all kinds of sleds in there, free for use on this slope."

Graham glanced up the tall hill. It had been a long time since he'd been on a sled. A long time since he'd been five. He couldn't be sure, but this slope looked too steep for two little girls.

As if she could read his mind, Faith spoke in a low tone. "It's really perfect. The snow is soft if they take a spill. And see how it is at the bottom? No trees, water or roadways to worry about. The worst part is climbing up there with the sleds."

Graham felt his daughters' eyes on him and knew they were begging just as hard as the boys, only in their heads. "Sounds like fun."

"Yay." The twins hopped up and down.

"Let's go pick out our sleds." Dustin slapped one of his boys on the back and slung an arm around the other while Krista beamed.

*Family.* It struck him then, and Graham wondered how he hadn't seen it. At the core, this was what defined this couple and was the key to their brand.

Thoughts of how he could incorporate this into their campaign began circling in his head as they picked out saucers and toboggans and snow tubes in the shed and began the long climb up the hill.

~

The two sets of twins ran on ahead, while Faith lagged behind with Krista. Dustin and Graham had fallen into conversation on the walk up, and Faith wanted to give him time to connect with Dustin.

Krista appeared to want this time alone with Faith as well. The pretty blonde, her blue ski coat making her eyes look even bluer, gestured with her head toward the two men who were now out of earshot.

"The coziness seems to have continued." Krista's tone held a lot of curiosity but no judgment.

"Graham is a good friend." Faith managed to keep her voice offhand even as she wondered what she'd done today to further pique Krista's interest. Not that her relationship with Graham was a secret or anything.

It was just because whatever this was between them was new and shiny and a whole lot personal, she told herself. She wanted to hold it close to herself for a little bit. She didn't want her friends analyzing and making more of it than it was or could ever be.

"I think there's more." Krista lifted a shoulder, then let it drop. "But if you don't want to say, I won't—"

"I slept with him."

Faith wasn't sure who was more surprised by the admission, her or Krista.

The blonde's eyes widened before she grinned. "That's fabulous."

"He'll be leaving at the end of the month." Faith wasn't sure why this was her response. She wished she'd said something cute and flippant.

Then again, she'd never been a cute and flippant kind of gal. But she hated making it sound as if she wanted more. She'd gone into this...this thing...with Graham with her eyes wide open.

It was just sex. Two consenting adults enjoying each other's company for a brief period of time. Faith just hadn't planned to fall for him. Or to find herself wishing for more.

"You might be leaving soon yourself," Krista said.

Faith blinked.

"If you accept our offer." Krista's hand touched her arm. "Please tell me you're at least considering it."

Crazy as it sounded, she hadn't given the offer a thought today. She'd been too busy mooning over Graham.

"I am definitely giving it consideration," Faith said quite seriously. "For many people, the opportunity to work with friends you love and admire and for your business to soar would be an opportunity of a lifetime."

"You're still not sure."

"I'm certain it's a fabulous deal. A wonderful opportunity. I just need to make sure it's right for me." Faith slowed her steps until they stopped, and Dustin's and Graham's coats soon became mere spots of color in the distance. "I've told you a little about my family."

Krista's expression had turned solemn. "The high achievers."

"Every last one of them," Faith agreed. "With the exception of me."

Faith held up her hand to stop Krista's protest. "I'm the slow-goer," she said, recalling Charlotte and Hannah's teasing words to each other, "rather than the go-getter. Money and prestige aren't all that important to me."

"You've made your decision." Krista's smile faltered, but understanding filled her eyes. "I respect that. I had hoped, but—"

"No." Faith shook her head. "I haven't made any decision."

Krista's brows pulled together in confusion. "You said that money and prestige aren't important to you. This opportunity offers both."

"While those things would be added perks, they don't motivate me." Faith struggled to explain something she didn't quite understand herself. "But the opportunity to have my work gain a wider audience, to employ more people, to bring more tourists to Holly Pointe. Not only that, I'd get to work with two people I love and admire. Those are potent draws."

"We'll need a decision by the end of the month, but you don't have to decide anything today." Krista started walking up the path, and Faith fell into step beside her. "In fact, I want you to take your time. If you're like me, you'll change your mind several times before you come to a decision that's right for you."

Faith wrapped her hand around Krista's arm and squeezed. "I'm glad we're friends."

"I am, too."

No other words were said until they reached the top of the hill. The boys, one on a red saucer and one on a blue one, were already on their way down the hill.

Graham was positioning the girls in the front of a long toboggan. When he saw Faith, his expression brightened. "You're just in time."

She smiled. "For what?"

"There's a seat on this bad boy," he gestured to the shiny sled, "and it's calling your name."

Not even a minute later, Faith found herself on the sled, behind the girls and in front of Graham as they shot down the hill.

"Yay," she called out from the sheer joy of it.

As if voicing her pleasure had given the girls permission, they yelled and screamed on the way down.

Graham's hands held tight to the rope as he steered a steady course.

Faith's heart pounded, and her breath came in short puffs by the time they reached the bottom.

The girls scrambled off the sled, their faces red and their eyes bright.

"That was super fun," Charlotte huffed out.

"I want to do it again," Hannah told her dad. "Only this time on one of those saucer things."

"Yeah, I want to go down by myself," Charlotte asserted.

"Well, I liked going down with your dad." Faith shot Graham a wink.

It was true. She liked feeling his body pressed against hers and his warm breath on the back of her neck.

"You can go down with him by yourself." Charlotte waved a hand like a queen bestowing permission.

The girls loved the saucers so much that the toboggan became Graham and Faith's. On what she knew would be their final trip down the hill, she leaned back against Graham and lifted her face to the sky.

When the sled came to a stop, his arms tightened around her as if he was reluctant to let her go.

The girls were soon engaged in a snowball fight with the boys. The scene, with its blue sky, ground covered in white and gales of laughter, was so heartwarming it brought tears to Faith's eyes. This, to her, was Holly Pointe. A place for families. A slower-paced environment where friends had time for each other and neighbors were there if you needed them.

*I wouldn't have this in Gatlinburg.*

Faith shoved the thought aside. She'd meant what she said to Krista. She would consider the offer, look at it from all angles before making her decision. Thankfully, she didn't have to make that decision right now.

Today, she would embrace the present without one thought to the future.

"We promised the boys burgers at Rosie's," Dustin was saying. "We'd love for you to join us."

Graham glanced at Faith, and she saw the question in his eyes.

"We've got Christmas bingo at the house today." Faith thought about the plans already firmly in place. "I believe Mary and the volunteers who are coming over can handle it."

"Fabulous news." Krista beamed.

"What news?" Hannah came over, her coat splotched with snow and her eyes shining.

"We're going to Rosie's Diner for burgers," Graham told her.

Hannah's gaze settled on Faith, and a hopeful gleam filled her eyes. "All of us?"

Faith took her hand. "Yep. Once we drop off the tree at the house and put it in water, all of us."

# CHAPTER THIRTEEN

"I think they've taken more naps since they've been here than in the last three years," Graham said later that afternoon, closing the door to the bedroom and following Faith down the hall to the sitting area.

Faith smiled. "Lots of fresh air and activity will do that to a child."

Graham dropped down on the sofa beside her, placing his arm around her shoulders. "The warmth of the café and a full belly helped."

"The burgers were excellent."

"Your friend Mel kept giving me the fisheye."

Faith laughed. "She did not."

"She did." His fingers toyed with her hair. "I think she's worried I'm going to break your heart."

"That's an odd thing to say."

He shrugged. "Maybe."

"The way I see it, what happens during this month you're in Holly Pointe is no one's business but ours."

Graham heard her say it, knew in some ways she believed it,

but he'd also seen how important her friends were to her. Regardless of what she might say, their opinions mattered.

"I don't want to hurt you, Faith."

"I don't want to hurt you," she responded and kissed him lightly on the mouth. "Let's make a pact here and now not to hurt each other."

He shifted and extended a hand. "Want to shake on it?"

Her brown eyes held a devilish twinkle that he'd have had to be blind to miss. "I've got a better idea."

Her lips met his, and his hand dropped, then stole around her, pressing her body against his. By the time they came up for air, they were both breathing hard.

"Okay," she said, her breath coming in little puffs. "I'd say that's sealed good and solid."

He grinned. "But to make sure—"

Faith put her hands on his chest in a gesture that told him she wanted him to keep his distance.

Disappointment surged, but he sat back.

"I could kiss you all night," she said. "But first, tell me about your conversation with Dustin. With the twins around and then Mary wanting all the details on the sledding when we got home, there wasn't a chance to ask."

*Home.*

Yes, Graham thought, this had begun to feel like home in a way that his apartment in New York never had. His gaze drifted to the undecorated Christmas tree. Would Faith stick around and help him and the twins decorate it when they woke from their nap?

First, they'd need to shop for ornaments, then…

"Graham."

He jerked his attention back to the woman sitting beside him, dressed in black stretchy pants and a shirt with a Santa Claus face, complete with googly eyes. How was it he found such a look so incredibly sexy?

Her hand now rested on his arm. "You don't have to tell me if you don't want to. Like I said, I was simply curious."

"It isn't that." He gestured toward the tree. "I was just wondering what I'd need to do to convince you to help us decorate the tree."

That impish gleam returned. "Another kiss should do it."

He could kiss her, and she wouldn't bring up his conversation with Dustin again. But Graham didn't want her thinking that he was keeping anything from her. He liked them both being on the same page.

"We discussed my previous ad campaign, the one I presented in New York." Graham kept his tone matter-of-fact, though he had to admit the feedback had stung. "He told me my presentation was slick and polished and likely would have been a hit with any number of *Fortune* 500 companies."

"But…" The eyes that met his were soft with understanding.

"I missed the mark by a mile." He shrugged. "Win some. Lose some."

"You haven't lost, though, right? You have this month to knock it out of the park."

"Correct." He grinned, then sobered. "Dustin wasn't able to articulate exactly what he and Krista want, other than they'll know it when they see it."

"That's helpful."

He chuckled. "It's pretty common. The one thing he said that was a repeat of the feedback I received before was that the ads and the overall campaign must stay true to their brand."

"Which is?" she prompted when he didn't continue.

"Which is what I'm trying to nail down." Graham felt himself settle and realized that talking this out with Faith was helping him make sense of it in his own head. "Today, seeing them at the Christmas tree farm with their boys, watching their interactions while sledding and later at the café had me seeing them in a new light."

He took her hand, smiling when her fingers curved around his.

"Family. It's important to them in a way I hadn't realized. They've done a good job of keeping the media coverage of the twins to a minimum." Graham absently stroked the palm of Faith's hand as he continued to speak. "That's what I think threw me."

Faith inclined her head and offered an encouraging smile.

"When the two of them are at galas or parties, they appear to be a high-powered career couple. Prior interviews dealing with her modeling career and his success on the ice led me down a wrong path. I really thought they wanted slick, when that isn't what they wanted at all."

"Have you seen their television show?" Faith asked.

"Only a couple of early episodes. That was a big error on my part." He expelled a long breath and started to pull his hand away, but to his surprise, she held on.

"Continue." She circled her free hand in a tell-me-more gesture.

"What I observed today was a couple who place high value on home and family." Graham shrugged. "I plan to watch several episodes of their show. I'm going to focus on the most recent ones to see how they've evolved and how they see themselves now."

"You're on the right path," Faith told him. "They may be all glitz and glitter at galas, but home and family are where their heart is, as well as giving back."

"You're so smart." His finger rose to trace a line down her cheek. "So sexy. So—"

"When are we going to decorate the tree?"

Graham dropped his hand, feeling like a teenage boy with a girl on the sofa and a parent in the doorway.

Instead of a parent, Charlotte stood there, blinking away the last of the drowsiness from her eyes.

She didn't wait for an answer, merely raced across the room and propelled herself into his and Faith's laps. Since they were sitting so close, it was difficult to tell where one lap ended and the other began.

"We're going to decorate the tree tonight," Graham told her.

Charlotte gave a little squeal. Flinging her arms around his neck, she gave him a noisy kiss on the cheek. "You're the bestest dad."

Graham's heart melted, simply melted.

"What going on?" Hannah ambled across the room and crawled into Faith's lap, wrapping one arm around her neck in a companionable gesture.

"We're decorating the tree tonight, Han." The words tumbled from Charlotte's mouth, excitement making them nearly unintelligible.

If the shout Hannah gave was any indication, she didn't have one bit of trouble deciphering her twin's words.

Hannah burrowed her head against the hollow in Faith's neck. "You're going to help, too, right?"

Faith glanced at Graham, and he formed the word *please*.

"Yes," she told the girls. "If you'd like, I'll even help you make the decorations."

"I've never known anyone who made their own tree decorations." Graham sat at the kitchen table and glanced at Faith.

"Focus." Faith gestured. "You're getting behind on your popcorn garland."

Graham picked up the blunt-tipped needle and began threading it through popcorn kernels. "I'm surprised they're not stabbing each other."

"You said nearly the same thing when they were using the glue gun to make the plaid bows." Faith had seen the worry in his eyes and understood. But she'd given classes to children this age and knew what they were capable of doing and what needed to wait until they were older.

"I realize I can be overprotective." He shook his head, a rueful smile lifting his lips. "What surprises me is their bows look a thousand times better than mine."

"Remember, it isn't about which ones look the best. We're making these decorations with love. That's what's important."

"I've never known anyone like you." His gaze settled on her, and her blood turned to molten lava.

She'd gone three years without sex and had never really given the lack much thought. Now, all she could think about was getting naked with Graham.

About making the most of the time they had left.

Because the thought of him leaving made her sad, Faith finished off her popcorn garland and clapped her hands. The girls immediately turned toward her.

"Once you and your father finish with the popcorn garland, we'll move on to our final project."

"What is that?" Charlotte's voice quivered. "The angel at the top?"

The hopeful note in her young voice had a lump forming in Faith's throat. She hoped they liked the angel she had in mind, but told herself if they didn't, she would work with them until they found something they did like.

"We'll get to the angel," Faith promised. "For now—"

She pulled a bag that she'd brought into the room with all the other supplies and upended it on the table. Pinecones scattered like pennies across the table covered in butcher paper.

Charlotte and Hannah exchanged puzzled glances. For that matter, Graham appeared plenty puzzled himself.

The girls' confusion turned to broad smiles when she brought out cans of spray paint. "We have silver, gold, red and green. There's enough cones here that we can each spray-paint four."

Hannah's hand shot up.

"Yes, Hannah?"

"Do we do one in each color?" The girl surveyed the aerosol cans. "Or can we—?"

"Whatever you want," Faith told her, including Charlotte in the instructions. "If you want to do all silver or green, that's your choice. If you want to do two of one color and then have the other two different, your choice."

Out of the corner of her eye, Faith saw Graham wince as she picked up one of the cans and demonstrated. "You need to spray toward the tabletop, not at each other or anywhere else in the room."

While they watched, she turned the brown cone into a shiny silver one.

"I want the silver," Charlotte said immediately, reaching for the can.

"I wanted the silver." Hannah's lips formed a pout.

"There's more than enough silver for everyone." Faith glanced at the cans. "I'm starting with the green."

The ugliest color, at least in Faith's estimation, but one she knew the others wouldn't want. For her, whatever colors her pinecones ended up being didn't matter. She was simply enjoying this time with the girls and Graham.

Faith had invited her grandmother to join them, but Mary had been tired after a busy day of bingo and had retired to her room. She hadn't appeared tired to Faith's assessing gaze, but energized. The bounce Faith had seen in Mary's step had warmed her heart.

The twins each took a can and began to spray, gaining confidence with each dash of paint.

Graham's red wasn't much prettier than Faith's green, but he appeared to be having fun.

"When I planned this trip," he spoke in a low voice, his words for Faith's ears only, "I hadn't given much thought to how I could make Christmas special for the girls."

Faith nodded. He didn't need to say more. She knew his plan had been to leave the twins with Ginny as much as possible so he could work on his campaign.

While he might have left them with their grandmother Friday night while he was at the party and let the twins assist Ginny with candy-making yesterday, Graham hadn't just dumped them on Ginny. He'd carved time out of his own schedule to make the holiday special for his girls. Together, they'd built a snowman, gone sledding and even tromped through the snow to pick out the perfect tree.

"It's funny how we have these dreams for ourselves and we're so sure of the path toward those dreams." She finished off her pinecone and set it aside to dry. "Then life throws us a curve ball, and we're given the opportunity to not only consider the path we were on, but whether the dream is still something we want."

"You understand." Surprise flickered in his green depths.

"You thought I wouldn't?" She kept her voice equally low as she reached for another pinecone.

"I wasn't sure." He glanced down at his red cone and grimaced.

"It's lovely," she assured him.

"Too much paint," he said.

"You'll get it right this time."

An emotion she couldn't quite identify flickered in his eyes. "I hope so. There's a lot riding on it."

# CHAPTER FOURTEEN

The girls went around the tree with what seemed like miles of popcorn garland until they were dizzy. Once they gained their equilibrium, they spent the next few minutes hanging lights and clipping plaid bows to the tree with clothespins.

Soon after Faith had headed downstairs with the promise of returning with a "special surprise," the twins started clipping the wooden clothespins on each other.

"This behavior tells me you're getting tired." Graham spoke in a stern voice. "Perhaps we need to wait until tomorrow to hang the pinecones and put on the tree topper."

Charlotte paused, clothespin open and ready to bite. She let it snap closed. "No. We're good. Aren't we, Hannah?"

Hannah dropped her clothespin into her pocket and out of sight. "We're good."

"Help us with the pinecones, Daddy," Hannah urged. "It's more fun when you help."

Charlotte gave a decisive nod. "Loads more fun."

After the craft part of the evening, Graham had held back, wanting his daughters to have the pleasure of putting all the ornaments and garland on the tree. The truth was, he was having fun watching them.

But he obligingly reached into the sack and began hanging the pinecones—thanks, glue gun—from the ribbon they'd glued onto the cones.

When Hannah placed three silver cones in the same area of the tree, Graham thought about mentioning it would be nice to stagger the colors. Then he realized they were having fun doing it their way. Wasn't that what this evening was all about?

He found himself whistling along with the Christmas music playing in the background as he hung the cones between the popcorn and bows. Hannah began singing under her breath, and he had to smile. From the time she could make noise, Hannah had sung little tunes when she was happy.

His heart filled to overflowing with love for these two precious girls. He and Steph hadn't planned on getting pregnant. Neither of them had been ready to be parents, but they'd made the adjustment.

What had Faith said? Something about adjusting your path? That's what had happened when the girls were born. He and Steph had gone down a different path, one that had given him two of life's biggest blessings.

"I love you girls." Graham realized he didn't say the words often enough.

"I know." A tiny smile tipped Charlotte's lips as she pointed at his chest. "And I love you."

"You're my daddy bear." Hannah wrapped her arms around him, snuggling close.

Graham's heart rose into his throat. How much he'd missed. How much he still would have missed if it hadn't been for Holly Pointe. If it hadn't been for Faith.

Her smile widened when she stepped into the room and saw him with the girls. She held a plastic sack loosely in one hand.

While still holding it, she lifted both hands and pretended to frame the tree. "This is such a lovely sight."

But she knew, and Graham knew, it wasn't the tree that had her eyes turning misty.

"What's in the bag?" Charlotte demanded.

"Is it the angel you promised?" Hannah looked up at Faith with hope in her eyes.

"I can't wait to see what you have in store for us." Graham crossed to her, surprising them both when he brushed a kiss across her cheek. "You've made tonight so special already."

If the girls found the kiss odd, they didn't show it. They only continued to clamor for her to open the sack.

Faith lifted a hand, stopping their questions. "Before I show this to you, I want to tell you a story."

Charlotte's gaze narrowed. "Then you'll open it?"

A chuckle was Faith's answer, but when Charlotte continued to give her the beady eye, she put a hand on the girl's shoulder. "Yes, after the story, I'll open it."

Faith gestured toward the sofa. "Shall we sit?"

Graham noticed Faith had barely dropped down when the girls took their places on either side of her. She shot him a barely suppressed smile when he was forced to take what little space was left.

"Once upon a time, long, long ago, when I was barely older than you are now, I lived in a big house with my parents and two brothers." She paused for a second as if memories clogged the telling, then resumed. "My parents were busy people, like your daddy."

"He's very busy," Hannah agreed.

"He's always working," Charlotte added.

Graham felt the pinprick of a knife blade in the area of his heart.

"My brothers were older and not into Christmas stuff."

Hannah's and Charlotte's eyes grew wide as they exchanged glances.

"Like your dad, we had a service that would come in every year and set up the tree. They would decorate it beautifully. Sometimes they'd have a theme and—"

Charlotte tugged on Faith's sleeve, stopping the story. "What's a theme?"

"It's like doing the tree in all blues and silver. Or like a peacock. Understand?"

Faith's tone, gentle and patient, had the young girl nodding.

"Well, while the trees were lovely, and I really, really liked some—"

Graham wondered if she'd really liked the decorations or if the "really, really liked" was a nod to him and his past Christmas trees.

"—when I'd look at the top of the tree, with its bows or feathers, or even one time a group of birds—"

That had the girls giggling.

"—I thought the tree needed something more. Because I was a child and didn't have money of my own, I went to my parents and asked if we could buy an angel for the top of the tree." Her lips lifted, but the flash of sadness in her eyes told Graham there was no happy ending to this part of the story.

"They bought an angel for you." Charlotte burst into a smile.

"That's the one you're showing us," Hannah added.

Faith shook her head slowly. "My mother said angels are lovely, but the service we used tried to avoid religious symbols, so they wouldn't have an angel."

The smiles of the twins turned to frowns.

Graham wasn't sure they understood what a "religious symbol" was, but if they had questions later, he'd clarify. For now, he listened as Faith continued with the story.

"I told her she didn't understand. I wanted her to buy an angel. One that we could put on the tree not just that year, but every year." Faith's voice remained steady as her gaze slipped to the tree.

The girls nodded as one, and Graham found himself nodding, too. He fought the urge to hurry her along and realized moving fast and making things happen quickly had become not only his lifestyle, but, well, him.

He took a deep breath, let it out slowly and told himself that, in this case, there was absolutely no need to rush.

"My mother shook her head." As if to demonstrate, Faith shook her own head and pasted a sorrowful expression on her face. "She said, 'I'm sorry, honey, but I don't have time. Besides, the tree is already decorated and you said you liked it.'"

"Did you?" Charlotte asked. "Like it, I mean?"

"I did."

"But it was missing an angel." Hannah leaned her head against Faith's shoulder and began to stroke her arm.

"Yes, it was missing an angel. So." This time, it was Faith's turn to take a breath and let it out. "I decided to make one. Our maid had a whole treasure trove of scraps and fabrics, and she helped me put together an angel. I thought she was the most beautiful angel in the world."

Everyone's gaze shifted to the sack, now sitting on the side table.

Hannah raised her hand. "I know the end to this story. The angel was on the tree every Christmas from that day forward. Amen."

Graham resisted—barely—grinning at that last word.

"Well..." Faith didn't answer immediately, and he could see that, once again, she was being careful with the words she chose. "My mother refused—ah, wouldn't put it at the top of the tree. She reminded me our tree had a theme, and the angel didn't fit that theme."

Charlotte sat up straight and crossed her arms, her lips forming a pout. "I don't like this story."

"Poor, sad little angel." Hannah's voice radiated concern. "She didn't have a tree."

Faith lifted a finger, and the smile on her lips reminded Graham of sun breaking through clouds. "Ah, but there is a happy ending to this story."

The girls studied her, said nothing and waited.

Graham held his breath. Until this moment, he hadn't realized just how much he, too, was anticipating a happy ending.

"Your mom changed her mind and let you put the angel on the tree," Hannah said before Faith could continue.

"Let her tell it." Charlotte frowned at her sister, then smiled up at Faith. "What happened?"

"I made a little tree out of green construction paper for my room. I put my angel on that tree." Faith's lips curved. "Every night before I went to bed, I'd look at her, and I'd feel happy."

"Nobody saw her," one of the twins said, but Graham was too busy looking at Faith's glowing eyes to notice which one.

He reached over and took her hand, giving it a squeeze.

"I saw her," Faith told the girls. "Every time I was in my room, I saw her. And Sharron, our maid who'd been so kind to help me make her, saw her. Even my family, if they happened to be in my room, saw her."

Graham had the feeling there was a lot more that Faith wasn't telling. Such as, perhaps the only reason that angel was allowed to live in Faith's bedroom was because very few saw it.

"Nice," Charlotte said.

"You brought her to Holly Pointe with you?" Graham asked.

Faith nodded. "She's with me wherever I live. Each Christmas, I bring her out, and she sits atop a special tree."

"Why isn't she downstairs?" Charlotte's brow furrowed. "You have big trees there."

"I think she's been waiting for a *special* tree." Faith's gaze shifted, and they all looked at their tree.

"We'll take good care of her," Hannah said. "You can come and see her whenever you want."

"You could even move in here with us, if you wanted," Charlotte offered. "That way, you could be with Daddy and us and see her all the time."

Graham avoided looking at Faith and sensed she was avoiding looking at him, too.

"I'm just downstairs so that will work, and I know that the three of you will take good care of her." Faith met each girl's gaze, and when her eyes shifted to him, he felt the punch.

"Daddy won't let anything happen to her," Charlotte assured her.

Hannah slipped her little hand in his. "Just like he doesn't let anything happen to us."

His heart suddenly became a thick mass in his chest. All this over talk of a homemade angel.

"Can we see her now? Can we? Can we?" Charlotte begged.

"We really, really want to see her," Hannah told Faith.

Graham held his breath when Faith rose and opened the sack. He thought of the type of creation the twins might make and hoped Faith's angel wouldn't be too big of a disappointment.

The girls gasped when Faith withdrew her angel.

For a second, he wondered if she'd switched her homemade angel for one she'd purchased in the store. But this one—with a sparkling tulle skirt of blue and pink and a glittery silver crown atop her head and a face that wore a broad smile—was totally Faith.

"That's amazing," he heard himself say.

"She's beautiful." Charlotte glanced at her twin, and Hannah nodded.

"Would you like to hold her?" Faith asked. "Before we put her on the tree?"

"She's old," Graham warned, visions of rough handling and a

treasure destroyed flashing through his head like lightning bolts. “Be very careful.”

Faith smiled and shot him a reassuring wink. “She’s sturdier than she looks.”

“We’ll be careful, Daddy,” Hannah told him, reaching out for the angel.

For once, Charlotte didn’t step in front of her sister or try to grab the angel out of her sister’s hands. She simply stood quietly at Faith’s side, with Faith gently stroking her hair, as they watched Hannah.

Hannah touched the tulle skirt with a gentle finger, then traced the smile painted on the face. “You’re going to like it on our tree.”

Then, with great reverence, Hannah held the angel out to her sister.

Charlotte gazed down at the angel in her hands, then lifted her gaze to Faith. “You make beautiful things. I wish I could make beautiful things out of scraps.”

“You can.” Faith’s gaze never wavered from Charlotte’s eyes. “I can show you how. Just like Sharron showed me all those years ago.”

Charlotte silently nodded, then held out the angel to Graham.

“I think Faith should put it on the tree.”

She studied him for a long moment. “How about we do it together?”

“Okay.” Why did he feel as if she’d asked him something that had nothing to do with placing an angel atop a tree, and he’d accepted?

Graham pulled to his feet, taking the angel from his daughter’s hands. So light, barely a whisper, yet filled with so much meaning and emotion.

He and Faith moved to the tree, the girls at their sides.

Graham gave a little laugh. “I feel as if I should give a little speech or something.”

No one else laughed. They only nodded as if waiting for him to say a few words. The trouble was, he didn't have a clue what to say when placing an angel atop a tree.

*Speak from the heart.* Wasn't that what Ginny had said when they'd been talking? Not about this, of course, but it seemed to fit. For now, it was the only advice that came to mind.

"This tree was found by those in this room on a wintry day filled with sunshine. We picked it out. We brought it here. Then we made decorations with our own hands and put them on this tree."

"It was fun," Charlotte said.

"Super fun," Hannah echoed.

"I had a blast." Faith nodded.

Graham smiled. "Now, we bring this angel, a symbol of a child's desire for something beautiful and personal and special, to top this Christmas tree."

As one, he and Faith lifted the angel and fastened her to the top of the tree, adjusting her until she was straight.

Graham wrapped an arm around Faith's shoulders as the girls clapped.

"We should sing," Charlotte told him.

"Gramma taught us a song." Hannah began to sing *Silent Night* in a sweet soprano that had emotion clogging Graham's throat.

He began to sing the words he'd known since childhood. And if his daughters got a few of the words wrong and made up some of their own, that made the moment only more special.

"Sleep in heavenly peace," they sang, ending the song in unison.

Graham met Faith's eyes. "Thank you."

Then he turned to his daughters. "Thank you, too."

"For what?" Charlotte asked.

"For making this a night I'll always remember."

# CHAPTER FIFTEEN

"I feel so close to him," Faith confided in Mel after telling her the story of what had gone on last evening. "And to the twins."

"You're falling in love with him." Mel spoke in a matter-of-fact tone as she handed Faith a piece of driftwood to inscribe. "I see it in your eyes, hear it in your voice."

"He doesn't fit anywhere in my life." The fact that she spoke the truth didn't stop Faith from wishing that he did, even though she knew she had to be practical.

Even seeing Graham and the girls head out for a day of skiing at Jay Peak with their family had had Faith wishing she could go with them. Their cousins were older, and the girls were beginners. Would they get left on the bunny slopes with an instructor with too many children to handle?

The second the thought entered her head, she dismissed it. The ski resort had excellent instructors. Besides, Graham would never let anything happen to the girls.

"I wish I could be with them."

Faith didn't realize she'd spoken aloud until she felt Mel's hand on her arms. "Where?"

Faith blinked. "What do you mean?"

"You said you wish you could be with them." Mel smiled. "Because I'm brilliant, I figured out that the 'them' you're referring to is Graham and his daughters. But where they are today is unclear."

"They went to Jay Peak with Shawn and his family. I believe Ginny even went, though I'm not sure if she still skis."

Melinda inclined her head. "Did they ask you to go with?"

"No." Faith shook her head more vigorously than the response warranted. "Why would they?"

"You like to ski."

"I do, but this is a family deal."

"You're kind of like part of the family."

Faith put down the finely tipped calligraphy brush. "You and I both know that isn't true."

"You want to be."

Expelling a breath, Faith gave up trying to work. Perhaps if she talked about the thoughts and emotions buzzing like a swarm of hornets in her head, she'd finally be able to concentrate. Right now, trying to work was an exercise in futility.

"Do you want to go for a walk?"

"Have you looked outside?"

"There's snow on the ground and more getting ready to fall." Faith rose and began cleaning her brush with precise, experienced motions. "There's always snow."

Melinda laughed. "Truer words."

"I've got some new snowshoes that I've been dying to try out. My old pair are still good." Faith wouldn't have asked if Melinda hadn't been dressed for an outing.

As her friend had grown up in this area, it was rare for her to be caught unprepared for whatever Mother Nature decided to throw at them. Which, according to forecasters, would be a blizzard by the weekend.

"After all the cookies and fudge I've eaten recently, I suppose it wouldn't hurt to burn some calories." Melinda, pretty as ever in a green cable-knit sweater that set off her peaches-and-cream complexion, rose and stretched. "Plus, I never realized how hard it is to work in a café and be constantly surrounded by food."

Faith laughed. "You're still a skinny minny."

"Am not."

"Are, too." The interchange reminded her so much of the twins that Faith's heart flip-flopped. "Let's get going before the snow starts again."

By the time Faith finished cleaning her brushes and she and Mel got the snowshoes on, small flakes had started to fall.

There was an area not far from the shop where Faith often went that cross-country skiers used. They headed in that direction now and stayed to the edge of the woods, away from the skiers' preferred path.

The sky had turned gray, and the sun seemed to be having difficulty breaking through the clouds. After yesterday's fun-filled magical day, the overcast seemed to match Faith's mood.

They strode along, settling into an easy rhythm developed only after much experience. Inhaling the robust scent of evergreen, Faith reveled in the tiny snowflakes on her face and the cool, crisp air. After several minutes appreciating the beauty that surrounded her, Faith felt herself settle.

"I am in love with him, Mel." Faith gave a little laugh. "I was with Thomas two years and was never sure I loved him. I've spent two weeks with Graham, and I'm sure. It's a heckuva thing."

"I wondered."

Faith couldn't believe Mel was showing such restraint. Normally, she was as tenacious as a badger, digging for details, asking question after question.

"You…wondered?"

Mel lifted a shoulder in a barely perceptible shrug, then placed her pole into the ground. "There's a look in your eye when you say his name. I'm surprised you're not shouting it from the rooftops."

"Yeah, that's my style."

They both had to laugh. Faith had never been one to talk about men. Maybe because she hadn't dated much since coming to Holly Pointe. Maybe because, as president of the chamber of commerce, she had an image to uphold. Or maybe it was because she was scared.

"I thought I knew Thomas." She heard the words tumble out, barely conscious of thinking them before they fell into the air. "I liked him, admired him and at one time thought we might have a future together. But then—"

Mel didn't fill in the blanks as she'd hoped, even though Faith had told this story before.

"Then Mary got sick, and I had to come take care of her."

"You wanted to come," Mel clarified.

"I had to come." Faith knew there was a subtle difference, but it seemed important. "Not *had to* in the sense that someone was making me do it. In fact, everyone was arguing the opposite. My family agreed that we should do as Thomas suggested and hire a medical professional to stay with her."

Melinda gave a snort. "As if she'd ever have agreed to that."

"Even if she'd been open to the possibility, I wanted to be with her." Love and fear and worry and all the emotions Faith had experienced when she'd heard her grandmother had fallen rose up in a tidal wave of emotion. "I wanted to care for her. When I was growing up, she showed me so much love. She always had my back. Unlike my parents, who had such high expectations, Mary only had one. She wanted me to be happy. When she needed me, I had to be there for her."

"I'm glad you came back," Mel said. "Glad I came back to run the café when my mom needed me. Otherwise, we never would have been friends."

*Another blessing,* Faith thought. Not only did she have a loving grandmother in this community whom she got to see every day, she had good friends.

If she were to relocate to Gatlinburg, she would lose all that meant so much to her.

"Now that we are friends," Mel said, "nothing will change that. No matter where you live."

Yes, indeed, her friend was perceptive. But this wasn't just about Dustin and Krista's offer, or about moving to Tennessee to build her business. It was about Graham. And the twins.

"I love his girls. As if they were my own." Faith realized that it didn't exactly fit with where the conversation had been going, but what she felt for Graham and his daughters was at the heart of her indecision.

"I'm sure the girls love you. Kids always love you." The eyes Mel fixed on her were filled with speculation. "Do you think Graham cares as much for you as you do for him?"

"It feels as if he does, though I could be simply confusing love with lust." She tried for a light tone, but her voice pitched too high.

"I was in a relationship like that, back when I lived in Burlington. I thought he loved me." Mel's tone gave nothing away. "He didn't."

Mel was more a closed book about what had happened in Burlington. Faith knew Mel had returned to help her mother at the diner, but something else had propelled her home, something darker.

Faith had left the door open for Mel to bring it up, but so far Mel had refused to step through it.

"Whatever decision you reach, Faith, whether it's to return to New York City with Graham or take the big-business leap in Gatlinburg, the decision needs to be made with what you want in mind."

"That's where it gets muddy." Faith threw up her hands, sending her ski poles pointed out like two spears ready for battle.

"I want Graham and the girls, though I'm not sure he's thinking long term. I want to expand my business, but I worry I'll end up in another dog-eat-dog environment like what I was in when I worked in New York. I love it here, genuinely love it here, but the thought of reaching more people with my inspirational messages and having more freedom to simply create excites me, too."

"Let's talk perfect world."

Faith glanced around at the green of the trees laden with snow, a herd of deer in the distance. "This is perfect."

"Yes, it is, but that's not what I meant." Mel shot her a look that reminded Faith of Miss Symonds, her fifth-grade teacher who hadn't put up with any shenanigans. "If this was a perfect world, and you could design your future, what would it look like?"

Though the snow continued to fall, and stopping their walk, even for a minute, didn't seem prudent, Faith paused to fully consider Mel's question. "In a perfect world, I would marry Graham and live here with him and the girls. Maybe have a few more babies. He would work remotely, as would I. I'd do the design work for Dustin and Krista and be the voice and face of Faith Originals, but on my time. I'd fly wherever I needed to go and then return home. To my friends and family."

"That's what I'd shoot for, then," Mel said.

"It's pie-in-the-sky," Faith told her. "It'll never happen."

"People reach their dreams by going for those dreams. They don't settle. They don't let things happen to them; they make things happen."

"I wish..." Faith didn't continue the thought, because a yearning deep inside her made it difficult to breathe, much less talk.

"That's how it all begins." Mel reached over and gave Faith's arm a squeeze. Her arm and Mel's mitten were both crunchy with snow. "With a dream and a wish. Go for it, Faith. What do you have to lose?"

~

If Graham had thought a day on the slopes would slow down the twins, he was mistaken. They chattered a mile a minute on the drive back to Holly Pointe.

"I'd love it if you could stay for dinner." Ginny, riding in the front seat of Shawn's large van, glanced over her shoulder. "Morgan should be home, so I'll start dinner right away."

"I hope she brings us a bunch of candy," Colten, one of the boys, said.

"She went to the Candy Cane House today," Shawn said. "So that's pretty much a given."

Cookie-making. Fudge. Candy. Graham's head spun as he thought of all the activities taking place under the massive roof. He wondered if Faith had been there today, helping, though she'd mentioned going into the shop to get some stuff done. Which reminded him of the campaign he'd put off while awaiting inspiration.

"We're having sloppy joes." Ginny smiled. "A favorite of the men in this car."

"I like 'em, too, Gramma," Charlotte told her.

"With pickles," Hannah said.

"I'd love to stay, but—" When he saw the joy on his daughters' faces fade, he clarified, "The twins can stay for dinner. This is a working vacation for me, and I haven't been doing much working. I have some business I need to attend to first."

Graham thought of the out-of-the-blue text he'd received from Dustin earlier today. They were to meet at the Busy Bean at five to discuss "business." A cold chill ran up his spine. If he lost this account…

He shook off the thought. Whatever it took, he told himself, he'd make it happen.

"Last night, we decorated the tree," Charlotte said for what had to be the zillionth time.

"Yeah, we heard." Colten groaned. "You put an angel on the top."

Charlotte's chin jutted out. "Not just an angel, a beautiful angel."

"Don't forget the part about how you sang around the tree." One of the boys in the back row—Graham wasn't sure which one, since all their voices had deepened—snickered.

"You're a poopy-head." Tears glistened in Charlotte's eyes, but she stubbornly refused to let them fall.

"Now, there's no need for name-calling." Graham wondered if this was what Tiffany dealt with every day. Probably not to this extent, since there were no older brothers.

It struck him again how far removed he'd been from the day-to-day. In the past couple of years, the nanny had been more of a parent to his children than he'd been.

Graham jutted out his jaw, mirroring Charlotte's earlier move. That ended now. When he returned to the city, he would take a more active role in his children's upbringing. Not simply because they deserved to have a father in their life, but because he wanted to be there.

# CHAPTER SIXTEEN

After reluctantly agreeing that the twins could not only stay for dinner but also spend the night, Graham left Ginny's house and drove to the Busy Bean. Snow now fell steadily in thick but small flakes.

The slick road conditions had Graham wondering if he should have called ahead. Would the coffee shop still be open?

As he drew close, he saw lights shining like a beacon through the plate-glass windows facing the street. Dustin's Jeep sat out front, covered in a blanket of snow. Graham wheeled his vehicle in next to it.

Bells jingled as Graham stepped into the building. The warmth was as much a welcome relief as was the hand Dustin raised in greeting from a table in the far corner.

After grabbing a cup of coffee, Graham crossed the room and pulled out a chair. "I don't envy you that drive back up the mountain."

Dustin only shrugged. With scruff on his cheeks and hair in need of a trim, he looked more like an NHL hockey player than a successful businessman.

"I'm glad you could make it." Dustin flashed a smile. "This shouldn't take long."

While his smile was friendly, something in the man's tone had an icy ball forming in the pit of Graham's stomach. He told himself not to jump to conclusions. He'd been given four weeks to come up with a new campaign, and the month was only half over.

Taking a long drink of his steaming brew, Graham ordered himself to settle. It must have worked, because when he spoke, his voice gave no indication of his inner turmoil. "What's up?"

"I like you, Graham. And, I must say, I appreciate a man who wants to get right to the meat of the matter."

Graham took another sip and waited.

"You and Faith have become pretty close since you arrived in Holly Pointe."

Obviously, this was merely a lead-in to talk of the campaign. Graham kept his tone offhand. "What's not to like?"

"I like her as well. My wife considers her a good friend. Which is where this gets tricky." Dustin blew out a breath.

Graham wondered if it was him, or was Dustin talking in circles? "I don't follow."

"Has Faith spoken to you about our offer?"

Tricky area. Was the deal supposed to be confidential? If it was, Faith had given no indication. "She mentioned your proposition."

Relief washed across Dustin's face. "I thought if you and she were as close as I thought that she would have. It's a great opportunity for her."

"It's an amazing offer," Graham agreed, wondering at the sudden chill creeping up his spine.

"It's a great opportunity for her," Dustin repeated, "but she's hesitating."

Graham sat back, fingers wrapped around the ceramic mug, and waited for Dustin to get to the point.

"I don't know why she can't see it." Frustration crept into Dustin's voice. "Perhaps you could help her understand this kind of deal doesn't often come around."

"I don't see why it matters." Then, deciding that might have been too blunt, Graham backpedaled. "I mean, it's not as if she's essential to your business."

In Graham's mind, them hiring Faith would be like finding an employee who fit. Dustin had to know that, in this day and age, there wasn't usually just one employee who fit, but many.

"That's where you're wrong. There's something about Faith. She firmly believes her inspirational messages and sayings make a difference." Dustin's expression softened. "She's what my grandmother would call 'good people.' You and I both know that while a person can possess inner goodness, that goodness doesn't always come across on the screen."

Graham nodded, reluctant to say more until he was certain where this conversation was headed.

"When Faith was on our show, ratings went through the roof." Mimicking Graham's earlier move, Dustin leaned back in his chair. His eyes remained as sharp as a shark's.

In that moment, Graham got a taste of what opposing players must have experienced when they tried to block this man's shot. When Dustin saw something he wanted, he was all in.

"I know Faith's work is important to her. Most of the time, to achieve this kind of deal she'd have to give up creative control, but Krista and I would never do that to her. We want her to always be her…just bigger." Dustin shook his head. "Faith doesn't seem to understand we're offering her the opportunity of a lifetime. She passes on this one, and she'll be stuck in this town forever."

Graham couldn't hide his surprise. "I thought you liked Holly Pointe."

"I do like it. It's like coming home when we're here over the holidays or on a ski vacation. The boys love the freedom of the small town during the summer, and my wife has dear friends here."

"Faith being one of them."

"Yes, Faith being one of them."

"What are you asking me to do, Dustin?"

"Like I said, you're a bottom-line kind of guy. So I'll lay it out for you." Dustin downed his coffee as if it were a shot of whiskey. "For the life of me, I can't figure out how to persuade Faith to accept what we're offering. I'm thinkin' you might be more persuasive. If you are, I won't forget it."

"Since I'm a bottom-line kind of guy, you'll need to spell this out even further for me."

Irritation flashed in Dustin's gray eyes. He was a good guy, someone Graham had liked instantly. Only now did Graham see he possessed that no-holds-barred, I'll-get-what-I-want instinct so prevalent in the business world.

That drive had served Dustin well on the ice and would serve him well as he and Krista continued to build their empire.

Leaning forward, Dustin rested his forearms on the table. "Convince Faith to accept our offer. I have no problems with her getting that attorney brother of hers to look over the contract and make changes. Bottom line, we want her on our team. Best for her. Best for us."

Graham lifted his cup to his lips, but didn't drink. "If I deliver?"

"I'll be grateful." Dustin waved a dismissive hand. "Don't worry about your ad campaign. If it's not exactly right, I'll let your boss know you're the man we want. We'll work together on it until it's something we can both live with."

"If I deliver Faith," Graham's tone was flat, "you'll approve my ad campaign."

Dustin shifted in his seat. "I don't know if I'd put it so bluntly."

"We're talking bottom line."

"Then, yes, that's the bottom line."

Graham inclined his head. "If I refuse?"

"Then I'll be disappointed."

If Graham expected Dustin to expand, he didn't.

"You say Krista considers Faith a close friend." Graham kept his tone even. "She's okay with all this?"

"Like me, she'd love to have Faith close." Dustin sat back again, his expression unreadable.

"I'm sorry to interrupt." Norma stood at the edge of the table. For a big woman, her steps had been as light as a cat's. "I wanted to let you know that we'll be closing in ten minutes. The storm isn't letting up."

Dustin glanced out the window at the same time as Graham. There wasn't much to see, as snow splatter now covered the glass.

Norma settled her gaze on Dustin. "I know you're probably eager to get home to Krista and the boys, but I worry about you heading up the mountain in this weather."

"Krista and the twins went to St. Johnsbury to visit a friend. With the storm moving in, she decided they'd spend the night." When a gust of wind rattled the glass, Dustin's dark brows pulled together.

"I've got a room upstairs you can use." Norma placed a hand on his shoulder. "Please stay. I'll worry myself sick, thinking of you on that road."

After slanting another glance at the window, Dustin didn't hesitate. "Thank you, Norma. I'll take you up on that offer."

"Good." She smiled at Graham. "You don't have far to go, and with the storm there won't be much traffic on the road, but I want you to drive carefully."

"No figure eights, I promise." Graham lifted a hand, his fingers forming the Boy Scout salute.

Her chuckle was followed by a laugh that came straight from the belly. "I'll hold you to it."

"We're just finishing up here," Graham told her.

Norma gave a nod, glanced at Dustin. "I'll ready your room."

"I didn't even hear her come up." Graham spoke in a low tone, his eyes on her retreating back. "Do you think she overheard?"

"Chill. We're not plotting a government overthrow."

Maybe not an overthrow, but *plotting* was still the right word. "Is your wife in favor of me pressuring Faith?"

"Krista wants Faith on our team." Dustin's voice held a hard edge. "But she doesn't know I'm speaking with you about this. There's no need for her to know. If you understand what I'm saying."

"I understand." Graham inclined his head. "What I don't understand is why me? There are lots more people in this town with more influence over Faith than me."

"You understand business." Dustin pushed back his chair and stood. "In business, like sports, when you want something, you go after it. I want Faith. Convincing her to accept the offer will be best for us, for her and for you."

Graham didn't see another car on the road during the short drive home. That was a good thing, considering the snow-covered roads and the fact that his mind was everywhere but on his driving.

Though he agreed with Dustin that this was a once-in-a-lifetime opportunity for Faith, the thought of pressing her to accept the offer made him uneasy. Still, would she regret turning her back on such a deal?

He recalled a time that Steph had turned down a position. A month later, when things had fallen apart at her firm, she'd been kicking herself for not fully assessing the offer and seizing the opportunity.

The fact that encouraging Faith to accept Dustin and Krista's offer would ensure he was awarded the ad campaign was something he preferred to not think about. Graham told himself that if he did encourage Faith to give the offer due consideration, it would be only because he didn't want her to end up with regrets.

As Graham turned into the freshly bladed driveway, he thought of Dustin's determination to have Faith on what he considered "his team." While Graham agreed Faith would be an asset, he suspected part of the reason Dustin was pushing so hard was because he didn't like being turned down.

It had to be the athlete in him, the part that said, *You tell me no, and I'll show you yes.*

Graham's chuckle had a hollow sound. He truly wanted what was best for Faith. He only wished that place was with him in New York.

The thought of returning to the city without her brought a fresh wave of sadness. While Vermont wasn't across the country, it was too far for quick weekend trips. If she chose Gatlinburg, she'd be even farther away.

Still, Graham believed the pace of Gatlinburg would be more Faith's speed. He could see her falling in love with life in Tennessee.

The words *falling in love* circled round and round in his head as he walked toward the house. By the time he reached the porch, he was forced to admit, if only to himself, that he'd fallen in love with Faith Pierson.

Graham wasn't an impulsive guy. He didn't fall in love in a couple of weeks. Especially not with a woman who wanted nothing to do with life in New York City.

He needed to face facts. He and Faith were like oil and water…

No. Graham shook his head. That was too simplistic. While it might describe their living preferences, he and Faith meshed on all other levels.

He thought about all Dustin was offering Faith. If anyone in his New York circle of friends had been presented with such an opportunity, they would have done a dance and immediately started packing.

But Faith, well, she wanted a balanced life, surrounded by family and friends. Could she have that life in Gatlinburg?

Graham had been to the town in the Smokies where Dustin and Krista planned to open their store and base their factory. Not only did Tennessee offer many business incentives, but the year-round influx of tourists made Gatlinburg a perfect location for the couple's new enterprise.

Had Faith ever been there? He could see them strolling down the quaint streets, listening to live music at the restaurants and doing a little moonshine-tasting.

The twins would enjoy hiking in the mountains and visiting Ripley's Haunted Adventure.

He saw it all so clearly.

Though he wished he could believe the trip would happen, he knew it wouldn't. Once he returned to the city, the twins would head back to their pre-K classes, and he'd dive into a mountain of work. Hopefully, he'd soon be celebrating the acceptance of his new-and-improved ad campaign...and his promotion to partner.

Despite the despicable weather, the thought made him smile. Though Graham wore gloves, he shoved his hands into his pockets and hunched his shoulders against the wind as he covered the last few feet to the door.

The second he stepped inside, the enticing aroma of chili wrapped around him. Like a hunting dog on high alert, he sniffed. In addition to the chili, were those cinnamon rolls he smelled?

Lunch suddenly seemed a distant memory. He slanted a glance into the front parlor, but found it empty. He saw remnants of a wrapping party that he hadn't realized had been on tap for this evening. Then again, it was difficult to keep all the activities straight.

He followed his nose to the kitchen. Graham hoped Faith

wasn't still at the shop. Perhaps he should have swung by there on his way home from the Busy Bean just to be sure.

His worry fell away when he spotted her at the stove, stirring a large pot of chili. If his nose was accurate, it was spicy hot, the way he liked it.

Cooling on racks on one counter were cinnamon rolls, the gooey caramelly kind, another personal favorite.

Instead of her normal holiday attire, which he'd grown increasingly fond of, Faith wore flannel pajamas covered in Christmas trees, with green edging at the ankles and wrists.

Thick woolen socks covered her feet. She hummed as she stirred. When his arms slid around her waist, she jumped.

Impulsively, he kissed her neck. "It's just me."

She relaxed back against him for a second. When she turned, she was smiling. "You could have ended up with chili all over you."

"A risk I was willing to take." He leaned over and, this time, kissed her slow and sweet on the lips. Graham knew he had to let her go, but brushed one more kiss across her lips before he released her. "Where's Mary?"

"She went to her room to do some cross-stitching and then to bed."

Graham frowned. "This early? Is she feeling okay?"

"She's good. In fact, I've never seen her better." Faith expelled a happy sigh. "The wrapping party shut down early because of the storm, but you should have seen her flitting from one table to the other, talking and laughing."

Graham wound a strand of Faith's silky hair around his finger and offered an encouraging smile, sensing she had more to say.

"She was the old Mary. The one I wondered if I'd ever see again." Tears sprang to Faith's eyes, and she sniffled. "Seeing her so energetic and happy is a dream come true."

"When you're happy, I'm happy." A rush of emotion had his voice turning husky.

He'd spoken the truth. Which was why he would not attempt to sell Faith on a life anywhere she didn't want to be. What made her happy would have to be at the heart of whatever advice he offered.

~

Faith set out huge bowls of chili and plates of large, gooey rolls. Conversation flowed inside as outside the snow continued to fall. Once they finished eating, Graham helped her clean up the kitchen. They took their after-dinner drinks of peppermint hot chocolate to the parlor.

Though she knew Mary would scold her, Faith put her stocking feet on top of the coffee table as she sipped the cocoa. "I'm glad the girls are spending the night at Ginny's."

"She loves having them all to herself." Graham relaxed against the back of the sofa. "The twins are crazy about those air mattresses."

Faith smiled. She liked knowing Graham valued family connections. She slowly stirred her cocoa with a peppermint stick. "How's the ad campaign coming?"

"Fine." Graham took her hand. "Great."

Well, that answered that question. Graham obviously didn't want to talk about his project. Which meant it was either going *fine* and *great,* as he'd said, or he was stuck. Faith made a mental note to bring up the topic again later.

Though she was no marketing or advertising guru, she might be able to offer a suggestion that would help him get unstuck, if that's indeed what was going on.

And, she considered, he might be able to help her get unstuck. Because that's where she was in terms of Dustin and Krista's offer—good and stuck. The pros and cons swimming around in her head reminded her of a kid treading water but going nowhere.

She knew Dustin and Krista wanted an answer. Faith also wanted to make a decision so she could move forward.

"I was wondering if you could do something for me." Perhaps it was her leaning close that had him jumping to the wrong conclusion. Or maybe it was when she set down her cup and took his from his fingers to set it down. If she had to venture a guess, she'd say it was when she scooted closer and wrapped her arms around his neck.

His fingers settled on her hips. The simple touch, even over soft flannel, had need erupting.

If the flash of heat in his green eyes was any indication, that need went both ways.

"Anything," he said, his voice raspy as she began scattering kisses up his neck. "I'll do anything for you, Faith."

When his mouth closed over hers and his hands slid up her sides to settle just under her breasts, she smiled. "Make love to me."

# CHAPTER SEVENTEEN

Graham took her hand, and they stumbled up the stairs. Though she wasn't sure why, Faith found herself laughing. Conscious of her grandmother sleeping downstairs, she tried to stifle her laughter, which only made her giggle.

After stopping to open the door at the top of the steps, Graham covered her mouth in a kiss that had laughter changing to a moan. Her breath came in short puffs as he pulled her inside his apartment, then caught when he scooped her into his arms.

Faith's heart gave a solid thump, knowing they were finally alone and wouldn't be disturbed.

One last giggle escaped her lips.

A smile quirked the corners of his lips. "I've never known anyone like you."

His approval, as warm and comforting as a fire on a cold winter night, wrapped around her. She trailed a finger down his cheek. "I bet you say that to all the woman who giggle their way to your bed."

"You, Faith Pierson, are a treasure and a delight." His gaze searched hers. "I find myself in the strange position of wanting to laugh along with you. Yet, at the same time, I want to make passionate love to you."

Faith couldn't stop herself. She giggled like a love-struck teen. "I pick door number two."

They tumbled onto his bed and, still laughing, fought to remove clothing with awkward hands. Kissing every five seconds didn't aid the effort.

Faith wanted him in a way she'd never wanted any other man. Finally, blessedly, the clothes were shed, allowing mouths and hands to roam freely.

Despite the urgent need, they didn't rush. The gentleness in his touch, the sweet words he whispered against her lips as he continued to kiss and caress, brought the love she felt for him flooding to the surface.

Faith climaxed, calling out his name, her nails digging into his back. Seconds later, Graham took his own release.

She cuddled against him, warm and sated, and her love for him filled her to busting.

Did he feel the same? It was easy to think he did when his hands stroked her skin with such care, and his warm breath caressed her neck.

Everything he did, everything he said made her feel cherished. Faith liked that, with him, it wasn't about what she'd accomplished or her material success, but simply because she was herself.

She wished, oh, how she wished, she could be with him forever.

The pang in her heart was a vivid reminder that one didn't always get what one wanted. Even in this most wonderful season of hopes and dreams fulfilled, there was still reality.

A strong gust of wind slapped the house and sent the windowpanes rattling.

Faith shivered, and Graham wrapped his arm even more tightly around her.

Snuggling against him, she chuckled. "At the moment, a warmer climate is sounding pretty good."

The hand that had been lightly stroking her belly stilled for a second. "Are you seriously considering the Tennessee offer?"

Faith liked to see someone's face when she spoke with them, but right now she was so warm and content, the thought of moving even a fraction of an inch held no appeal. "Does that surprise you?"

"A little."

Faith felt her lips lift. "Mary has always teased that while I pretend to be laid-back, in truth I'm just as driven as the rest of my family."

Graham brushed a kiss against her hair, and her heart swelled. "Is she right?"

"She's exaggerating." Faith expelled a contented sigh. "Though I admit I have worked hard to build a successful business."

"Mary is your biggest cheerleader." He tightened his hold on her. "Next to me, that is."

"I mentioned how much I'd hated living in Manhattan—"

She stopped abruptly when the arm around her shoulders stiffened. "I'm sorry. I wouldn't want anyone dogging Holly Pointe. You love the city. Lots of people do. There were parts of my life there I enjoyed. All the people and noise just weren't for me."

"I understand."

Faith wasn't sure how she'd expected him to respond, but disappointment surged. Couldn't he have at least asked her if she liked it well enough to come and visit sometimes?

He probably knew how difficult that would be for all of them. Going to his apartment, seeing him and the twins and then having to leave them would be brutal.

She thought of Charlotte and Hannah and how much she'd grown to love them. No, Graham had it right. No promises of more. A clean break after Christmas would be best for everyone.

"Have you ever been to Gatlinburg?" Graham asked.

"I've been to Nashville."

"A great town," Graham conceded, "but the two are quite different. Nashville is more of a city, while Gatlinburg reminds me of Holly Pointe. It's bigger, of course, but retains a small-town feel."

"Sounds more like my kind of place."

"Maybe. Hard to know until you've seen it. If you're seriously considering Dustin and Krista's offer, you might want to fly there and check it out. Then you can make sure it's a place where you could see yourself living. Or not."

Faith found herself frowning, though why exactly she wasn't certain. "I wouldn't want to waste everyone's time unless I was certain I wanted to live there."

"No way to know for sure until you see it, walk the streets, check out the housing options."

"Good points." Faith rested her head against his arm. This was a strong man, one she could count on to have her back. "The problem is they want an answer by the end of the year. I can't make a trip happen that quickly."

"They can't really expect you to make this decision without checking out the town, and they have to understand you can't go between now and Christmas."

"I suppose I could ask for more time…"

"You could get your contract changes ready, but save the final decision until after the trip." His palm continued to make slow circles on her belly. "Do you have other concerns?"

Faith might not have had the opportunity to write out her pros and cons, but a list had already formed in her head.

"I'd miss my friends. And my grandmother." She gave a little laugh. "Of course, we're not living in horse-and-buggy times. It's probably, what, a three-hour flight?"

"Sounds about right," he said. "Nothing says you couldn't fly back frequently. The Knoxville airport is close, and you'd be back in Holly Pointe, like you said, in a matter of hours."

Nodding, Faith thought of other items on her cons list. "I'm willing to work hard, but I don't want my job to be my life."

"That's why, when you review the contract, you make certain the terms are something you're comfortable with." Graham paused for a long moment. "It sounds to me as if they really want you. That puts you in the driver's seat."

"I know." Faith expelled a breath. "But I love my life here."

"I'm not telling you to walk away from it." Graham's voice took on an urgency. "You should do what makes you happy. Just keep in mind that happiness can look more than one way."

"For the record, everything you've said is something I've already told myself." Faith pulled her brows together. "I don't want to give the impression I'm some silly person who needs someone to tell me what to do or think."

He brushed a kiss against her hair. "I'd never think that of you."

"I like being able to bounce my concerns off you." Warmed by his caring, soothed by his touch, Faith closed her eyes and savored their closeness.

"I want to help." His voice, low against her ear, sent a shiver up her spine. "Are there others? Concerns, I mean?"

She fought to think as his nearness short-circuited her brain. "Ah, mostly things like making sure I have the creative freedom I need and that I retain the rights to the products I develop. That's where Bryce comes in."

"Bryce?"

"My brilliant brother. He has the kind of lawyerly experience I need. Because he's family, I can count on him to have my best interests at heart." Faith placed her hand over his. "It's the same with you."

"Me?"

"Like Bryce, I know you have only my best interests at heart."

~

After leaving Faith in the morning, Graham's plan was to pick up the twins, head straight back to the house and get some work done. But when he pulled up, the girls were in the middle of building a monster snowbear with their cousins.

With Shawn and Morgan at the grocery store, Ginny appeared determined to ply him with coffee and the doughnuts she'd picked up yesterday.

"I'm glad the girls stayed here last night." Ginny poured Graham a cup of coffee, then sat back to enjoy her own. "I wouldn't have wanted them on the road in such bad weather."

Graham lifted his cup. "Thank you, again, for keeping them."

Ginny smiled. "It warms my heart to see the twins getting better acquainted with their cousins."

Another thing to add to his should-have-done plate, Graham thought. He'd known money was tight for Shawn. Why hadn't he made the trip to New Hampshire with the girls at least once during this past year? Even as he asked himself the question, Graham knew the answer. He'd been too wrapped up in his own career.

While a single-minded devotion to business was the norm in his group of friends, this trip had reminded him of the need for balance.

Encouraging Faith to take her time before signing any contract had felt right. Faith wouldn't be happy if her private life ended up being taken over by work.

"Graham."

He blinked and found Ginny staring at him. Shaking his head to clear out the cobwebs, he smiled and took a long sip of the dark roast. "I believe I needed this more than I realized."

Ginny's lips lifted in an impish smile. "When I spoke with Mary this morning, she mentioned you and Faith stayed up pretty late last night."

Graham kept his face expressionless. Mary had been asleep—or so he and Faith had both assumed—when he'd gotten home. He thought of how tempted he'd been to make love to Faith in front of the fire.

She'd looked so pretty with the light from the flames turning her hair golden brown. Her pajamas had been incredibly soft. Thank goodness he'd waited until they were upstairs and behind closed doors to take them off.

"After we ate dinner, we sat in front of the fire, talking and drinking hot cocoa," Graham added when he realized the silence had lengthened. "Hot times in the old town."

A hint of a smile remained even as Ginny's assessing gaze pinned him. "You like her."

"Faith? Or Mary?"

The sharp look Ginny shot him had Graham grinning. "I like Faith a lot. What's not to like? She's smart, funny and talented."

"Do you love her?"

For a second, Graham wondered if he'd imagined the question. Surely Ginny—Steph's mother, for goodness sake—wouldn't ask such a personal question.

But when he met her gaze, Graham realized, well, yes, she had asked that question.

"I do." He kept his tone matter-of-fact, though saying the words aloud made his feelings more real. He'd nearly confessed his love to Faith last night.

Even if she loved him back, which he felt down to his bones she did, that wouldn't change the fact that his home was in Manhattan, and hers was, well, hers was either in Holly Pointe or Gatlinburg.

"Don't you think you should tell her how you feel?" Ginny's quiet question was really more of a comment.

"How do you know I haven't?"

"I know you." Ginny wrapped her fingers around the mug in front of her and gave him a long look.

The concern in her eyes only added to Graham's discomfort. A man's current love life wasn't a topic usually discussed with a former mother-in-law, even if that man felt closer to her than to his own mother.

Graham cleared his throat. "I don't see the point. My job is in New York City. Faith has made it clear she has no great love for the hustle and bustle of Manhattan."

"You could live in New Jersey. Or Connecticut. You could ride the train into the city, and she could have the country life she likes."

"Yes, but—"

"It's an option. It could be a compromise that allows the two of you…and the girls…to have a family life."

He hadn't considered moving out of the city and commuting…and why hadn't he? "She'd have to move her shop."

Ginny leveled those blue eyes at him. "It's primarily an online business."

Graham expelled a shuddering breath. "You're right. It's an option worthy of exploration."

"I hear she's got a chance to go big and move to Tennessee. Work with Dustin and Krista."

News traveled fast, he thought in amazement, and accepted that was small-town life in a nutshell. Not fair, but was it fair that Faith would be hounded by people wanting to know what she'd decided when she was still mulling options?

Graham thought of Dustin's deal, and a cold chill slithered up his spine. What if Faith heard about that proposition? He hadn't accepted Dustin's offer, yet he hadn't refused it either.

Had he given the impression he'd go along, hoping if Faith decided to go to Tennessee, Dustin would conclude it was because of his influence? Graham snorted in disgust. At Dustin. At himself. At this whole screwed-up situation.

"Graham."

Sick at heart, he looked up to find Ginny's concerned gaze on him. "Won't you tell me what's troubling you?"

His defenses crumbled under her motherly concern. "I love Faith, Ginny. But I feel like I can't truly put my self-interest aside to advise her."

"Why do you have to?" Ginny leaned forward, her bright blue eyes never leaving his face. "You need to be open to alternatives."

Graham laughed. "That's just what I was telling Faith."

"Well, then, follow your own advice. It's not a question of NYC vs. Holly Pointe vs. Gatlinburg. It's a question of together or apart. You're a creative guy, so get creative."

"You're right." His voice shook with emotion he couldn't contain. "I need to start thinking outside the box."

Ginny patted his arm, then surged to her feet. "Let's check on the children."

With Ginny at his side, he strode to the front window. Graham frowned. "The bear is still only half done."

"They're going for a grizzly. A big one." Ginny's lips tipped in a fond smile. "Those take time."

Graham's phone buzzed. It was a text from Faith.

*Hank can't make it in. Any chance you could help me get packages ready for pickup ASAP?*

Sensing Ginny's curious glance, he held out the phone so she could read the text.

"Hank Dumfries lives in the country on a low-maintenance road. I'm not surprised he couldn't make it into town. The plow probably won't get to him until tomorrow."

"That answers one of my questions." Graham studied the text. "What's this about getting packages ready?"

"I assume those are orders that need to be readied for the carrier to pick up so they get out on time." Ginny tapped her lips. "It could be anything from slapping shipping labels on boxes to putting items into the packing boxes. Whatever is going on, Faith needs your assistance."

Graham glanced out the window.

Charlotte and Hannah had taken a break and were making snow angels in the yard.

"They'll be fine." Ginny patted Graham's arm. "Who knows? That bear just might be done by the time you get back."

# CHAPTER EIGHTEEN

The seconds until Graham responded felt like hours. There were lots of people Faith could have contacted, but most of them would still be digging out.

Her own street, one of the more highly traveled in town, was always cleared early. Mel's brother had arrived first thing that morning to scoop the driveway and walks.

Taking care of each other was something that came naturally to people in this region. It was only one of many reasons she loved it here.

What she didn't love, she thought, slapping another label on a box, was work left undone. According to the note Hank had written to her, he'd left early yesterday for a family get-together. The note said he'd be in first thing to finish up.

Hank had lived in Holly Pointe his whole life. He'd known, just like everyone else in town, that a big storm was moving in.

Not only hadn't he finished his work, he'd left a note instead of calling her.

At the ding, she glanced at her phone. She expelled the breath she hadn't realized she was holding. Graham was on his way.

The fact these orders would, hopefully, now be ready for the carrier didn't negate that she'd been left scrambling and Graham had been inconvenienced. She and Hank would have a discussion about this when she saw him next.

When Graham knocked on the back door, the one that led directly into the work area, she motioned him inside.

Despite the cold, there was a lightness about him that she hadn't seen before, a spark in his eyes that made them glow like emeralds.

"Thanks for coming."

"A pretty woman texted she's dying to see me." He shot her a devilish smile. "How could I say no?"

"I didn't say anything about dying to see you." Still, her lips curved at the teasing banter.

"Subtext." He took the label from her hand, set it down, then pulled her to him for a kiss.

It was one of those kisses that started out slow, then, oh mama, left her barely able to form a coherent thought when it was over. She let herself lean, just for a second, against him.

Then, reminding herself there was work to do, she straightened. "Thank you for coming."

"You're welcome." He grinned. "Tell me what to do."

Graham caught on quickly. Which was good, considering there wasn't much time. They worked in silence.

Faith had just placed the label on the last box when a brisk knock sounded at the door.

A man in a steel-gray parka stepped inside. Faith fought to recall his name. Stan, yes, his name was Stan. He was the fill-in for her regular guy.

"We've got everything ready for you." With a sweep of her hand, Faith gestured to the boxes.

"Looks like business is good." Stan hefted an armful of boxes.

Faith smiled. "Gotta love Christmas."

"Let me help with those." Graham scooped up more boxes and

followed the man to the large utility van parked, its engine running.

In minutes, the rest of the boxes were loaded, and Stan was on his way to his next stop.

Faith dropped down on a stool. "Thank you so much. I couldn't have done it without you."

"Two sets of hands are always better than one," Graham quipped, even as something Ginny said resurfaced.

*A question of together or apart.*

Now that the boxes were gone and they were alone, Graham realized the time had come to speak from the heart and confess his love. "Faith, I—"

"I know what you're thinking. If I was in Gatlinburg, I wouldn't have had to do any of this." Faith's lips lifted in a rueful smile as she surveyed the room. "I could concentrate on what I love."

Swallowing the words poised on his lips, Graham expelled a breath. "Such as?"

"Designing new products. Being the face of Faith Originals on their show." Faith's expression grew thoughtful. "I received the contract this morning. I read through it, then sent it to my brother."

Graham couldn't hide his surprise. "You decided to accept?"

"Not yet." She traced a finger across a tabletop covered in a light coating of sawdust. "I'm still considering."

"It has to be appealing, the idea you could simply create and not have to worry about this." He gestured toward the packing supplies and boxes.

Graham started to say more but changed his mind. He would not attempt to influence her.

"When we talked the other night, several things you said hit home." She dusted off her hands. "This is an amazing offer, truly a once-in-a-lifetime opportunity. I'd be foolish not to give it careful consideration."

He settled for a nod.

"One thing holding me back is the lack of a social network in Tennessee." Her brows furrowed. "I don't have any family or friends there. Nobody even close."

*Krista and Dustin will be there,* he wanted to say, but Faith already knew that. Since she appeared to be waiting for a response, he simply said, "Having family and friends close by is important to you."

"It is. I believe having a healthy social life is a big part of being creative."

Again, she looked at him and waited.

Graham kept his tone matter-of-fact as he recalled their earlier conversation. "You could come back to visit. Your friends could visit you there."

"That wouldn't be enough." Faith shook her head. "I don't want to settle for a part-time social life. I want to live and work surrounded by people I love."

While Graham had hoped for a long-distance romance, he realized that would never be enough for Faith, and he wouldn't ask her to settle for less.

"Oh my goodness, Graham. You were picking up your girls this morning." Her voice rose, mirroring the distress on her face. "I'm so sorry. I should have reached out to someone else."

Before she even finished, he was shaking his head. "I'm glad you texted. The twins weren't ready to leave. They were..."

Graham went on to tell her about the huge "grizzly" the girls and their cousins were building in Ginny's front yard. "They love being at Gramma's. It's a special time for her and for them."

"Speaking of special." She stepped close and walked her fingers up his sleeve. "Last night was special for me."

"For me as well." His voice came out raspy. Graham paused to clear his throat. "I have something to ask you."

A watchful waiting filled her dark eyes. "What is it?"

"Are you planning on attending the Mistletoe Ball this Saturday?"

"It's the town's biggest holiday event." Her voice remained light, though for a second he swore he saw disappointment flicker in her brown eyes. "I never miss it. Will you be escorting Ginny?"

Graham took her hand and brought her fingers to his lips, his gaze never leaving hers. He might not be able to be a permanent part of her life, but he vowed to make this date one they'd both remember. "There's only one woman I want to take to the ball. Will you go with me, Faith?"

Deep in concentration, Faith jumped when her phone buzzed that evening. Bryce's name popped up with a FaceTime request. She pushed aside the rough sketch of an umbrella, raindrops and a saying about dancing in the rain, and accepted the request.

"Bryce." Pleasure rang in her voice. "I didn't expect to hear from you so soon." With December twenty-fifth just over a week away, it was too early for her brother's yearly Christmas phone call. And she'd sent him the contract only that morning.

Though the sun had set almost three hours ago, Bryce was still dressed in a dark suit, crisp white shirt and red tie.

It didn't surprise her that he hadn't gone home from work yet. He gave one hundred and ten percent to anything he did. The oldest child in their family, this boy who excelled at everything had been a tough act to follow.

Faith wondered how Bryce refilled his well.

"I finished the review of the agreement—" His dark brows pulled together. "Is that a *possum* wearing a Santa hat on your shirt?"

Faith looked down at her shirt, then back at him and grinned.

"The local Wildlife Rescue sold these as a fund raiser last

year." While opossums weren't the prettiest of animals, the one on her shirt had a sweet face. "Were you aware possums kill rats and cockroaches?"

Bryce lifted a hand, a pained look on his face. "Faith. I don't have time to discuss possums."

"I understand." She made her tone as brisk as his. "I appreciate you taking the time to go through this. I know you're busy, so let's get down to business. What are your thoughts?"

"I was happy to help." His voice had gentled, as if he'd realized how curt he'd sounded. "As far as thoughts, I'm impressed."

"By?" she asked cautiously.

"This is an amazing deal." Bryce gazed at her with admiration. "You're hitting the big time with this one."

*I'd never have thought it of you.*

Though her brother didn't say it, she knew that's what had him looking at her in a different light.

"Back to the contract." She shifted, decidedly uncomfortable with his approving gaze.

"I have a couple of suggestions. Nothing huge, but—"

As he requested, she brought up the document on her laptop. They went through each section together, with him pointing out a couple of areas where he felt the wording should be tightened.

"When will you be making the big move?" Bryce relaxed back in his leather desk chair, obviously deciding he had time for non-possum-related talk.

"I haven't yet decided if I'm going to accept the offer." Faith felt the weight of decision pressing against her chest. "I'm supposed to give Dustin and Krista my answer by the end of the month. I'll be asking for more time."

Bryce's dark eyes bore into hers. "You're foolish if you don't accept."

"I recall you telling me I was a fool for coming to Holly Pointe." Faith kept her tone light. "Which is interesting, considering it was here that I got to know Dustin and Krista on a personal level. It was here that they became acquainted with my art. That would never have happened if I'd stayed in the city."

"Touché." The dimple in Bryce's cheek, the one she hadn't seen in years, flashed. "You do what's best for you. If you decide to accept the offer, ask them to make the changes before you sign the agreement."

"I will. Thanks again."

"Tell Gram I'll call on Christmas."

"Absolutely." As Faith clicked off the call, she smiled, thinking Bryce probably already had the reminder set on his phone.

Getting the contract reviewed was one more step on the road to Gatlinburg, Faith thought, as she closed her laptop.

Tomorrow morning, she'd meet Krista for coffee at her house. Dustin was planning to take the boys skiing, which meant she and Krista would have the house to themselves.

Faith had a plan. Over coffee and scones—with Krista, there were always scones—she'd express interest in the position and request more time to deliver her decision.

Rising early, Faith dressed for a cold, wintry day in flannel-lined denim pants and a red cable-knit sweater. Because of a forecast wind chill of minus eighteen, she added a thermal undershirt beneath the sweater and two layers of socks.

Krista had already called early that morning to confirm the time. Once again, she emphasized they'd be alone. It had been a strange conversation. First, because Krista had called instead of texting, her normal method of communication. Then, there'd been a kind of hitch in her friend's voice that had Faith's Spidey senses tingling.

Telling herself she was being ridiculous, Faith slipped on her boots and studied herself in the mirror. Because she knew—hoped—she might run into Graham on her way out the door, she'd taken extra time with her makeup. She even brought out the big guns—her new red lipstick—to add an extra splash.

Even though she and Graham didn't have solid plans, they rarely went a day without seeing each other. Soon, that wouldn't be the case. They'd never really spoken about what would happen when he returned to the city. They'd spoken only about whether Faith would move to Tennessee.

She assumed that was because Tennessee was the only variable. Whether Faith was there or in Holly Pointe, it didn't change the fact that Graham had a life in New York. A city where he'd found success, where he'd made a home with his wife, where his children had been born. A city he loved as much as she loved Holly Pointe. She would never ask him to leave there, so what was the point of discussing it?

Faith closed her eyes at the thought of never seeing Graham and the girls again. Oh, she might run into them if they all happened to be in Holly Pointe at the same time, but it wouldn't be the same. It would never be the same.

*I'm strong,* Faith told herself. *I'll get through this.*

One way was to focus on next steps.

She would discuss with Krista the contract changes Bryce had suggested so the couple could have their attorney review the proposed changes while Faith visited Gatlinburg. That way, if she decided to accept their offer, there shouldn't be a delay in making Tennessee her new home.

"Mary," Faith yelled as she tossed a scarf around her neck and lifted her coat from the hook. "I'm heading out."

Instead of calling out a good-bye, Mary appeared in the foyer.

"I'm sorry you'll miss the gingerbread house competition." Mary tied Faith's scarf, and the fussy, maternal gesture had Faith's heart lurching. "Still, I like seeing you getting out and socializing with friends."

Faith slipped her arms into the parka and zipped up. "By the way, I spoke with Bryce last night. I'm supposed to tell you he'll be calling on Christmas."

"Bryce is a good man who works too hard. I'll be sure and mention the need for balance when he calls, just like I do every year." Mary's lips curved. "As your brother enjoys his law practice, I won't push too hard."

"I had him review the Gatlinburg contract."

Though Mary knew all about the offer, until now Faith had avoided bringing up the subject.

Mary lifted a brow. "You've made your decision?"

"I'm going to visit Tennessee after the holidays and check out the area." Faith paused. "I won't make any decisions before then."

"What does Graham say about all of this?"

Faith cocked her head.

"Don't play coy with me, girl. You and Graham have gotten close during his time in Holly Pointe." Mary's eyes twinkled. "I don't believe for one second this whirlwind romance will end when he returns to New York."

"We've spoken about the job offer." Faith chose her words carefully, trying to gauge Mary's thoughts. "Graham is actually the one who suggested I go there in person and check out the area before making any decisions."

"Did I hear my name?"

Faith turned and saw Graham striding across the parlor toward them, the twins at his side. "I was telling Mary about my plans to go to Tennessee."

Picking up the pace until they were running, the girls rushed to her.

Charlotte's face brightened. "Are you going to see Tiffany?"

"Can we come with?" Hannah asked.

A rush of emotion had Faith wrapping an arm around each girl. "I'd love to take you both with me, but I'm afraid this is a business trip."

Charlotte's expression fell. "Will you see Tiffany while you're there?"

Confused, Faith slanted a glance in Graham's direction.

"Who is Tiffany?" Mary asked.

"Our nanny," Hannah shouted, as if afraid her sister would beat her to the answer.

"She's in Nash-a-ville right now." Charlotte sang the words.

Her mommy and daddy live there," Hannah piped up.

"And her sister," Charlotte added. "Tiffany's big sister is getting married."

"That's exciting." Faith offered a smile. "I'd love to meet Tiffany, but I bet she'll be back in New York with you by the time I go there."

Charlotte's brows pulled together. "Aren't you going to be in New York with us?"

"Honey, New York is *your* home. I live here, in Holly Pointe." Faith stopped just short of promising to come to New York to see her and her sister. And see Graham, whose face was now an unreadable mask.

Small arms wrapped around her from both sides, encasing her as tight as any straitjacket. Though Faith was certain there wasn't a straitjacket on earth that would feel as sweet.

Tears pushed at her lids, but she blinked them back. "I saw the smiles on your faces this morning. Where are you and your daddy headed?"

It was an easy assumption to make as the girls and Graham already had on their coats.

"We're cel-e-brat-ing." Hannah wrung each syllable out of the word.

"Daddy got his project done." Charlotte smiled up at her father. "It's really, really good."

"The other one was stinky." Hannah pinched her nose with her fingers, as if smelling something foul, before dropping her hand to her side with a grin. "He got a do-over."

"Sometimes you need a do-over," Charlotte advised with a sage nod.

Faith shifted her gaze to Graham, whose eyes danced with amusement, and lifted a brow. "It's done?"

"It is," he confirmed, flashing a smile that had her insides fluttering. "In honor of the occasion, I'm taking the girls out for some good ol' diner food. Would you—"

"Daddy says we can get a muffin if we want," Charlotte announced. "I want one with blueberries."

"I like blueberries," Hannah admitted. "But I really, really, really want chocolate chip pancakes."

"What I was about to ask before I was interrupted," Graham's smile was indulgent, "was if you ladies would care to join us? My treat."

"I'd love to, Graham." Regret filled Mary's tone. "But this is Gingerbread House Day, and I need to be here."

"Can I help with anything?" he asked immediately.

Faith's heart warmed, as she knew the offer was sincere. Graham would defer his celebration plans with his daughters to assist Mary.

"I appreciate the offer." Mary patted his arm. "It's under control. All that's missing are the gingerbread house makers."

"I want to make a gingerbread house." Charlotte tugged on his arm. "Please, Daddy."

"Me, too." Hannah added her voice to the pleading.

"If you're interested, I've got a space for you and the girls." Mary's warm smile encompassed Graham and the twins. "You've got plenty of time for breakfast, as things won't get rolling for at least another hour. Even then, you can start whenever you get back."

Graham hesitated. Taking in his daughters' pleading expressions, he smiled. "Count us in."

Ignoring the girls' cheers, Graham shifted his gaze to Faith. She felt the familiar jolt when those green eyes met hers. "Can I interest you in breakfast at Rosie's Diner? I promise strong coffee and scintillating conversation."

"I'd love to join you." Faith hoped he could see the regret in her eyes. She sincerely wanted to spend as much time as she could with Graham and the twins before they left. "But—"

"Now, why did I sense there was a *but* coming?"

His teasing tone had her smiling. "Krista beat you to the punch. She already invited me to her house for coffee and scintillating conversation. Dustin is taking the boys skiing. Oh, and before you ask, the road to her place has been freshly plowed."

Surprise lit Graham's green eyes. "Derek works fast."

"That's why they pay him the big bucks. I need to go." Faith plopped a kiss on top of each girl's head, then brushed a kiss across her grandmother's cheek.

She planned to bypass Graham, but he stepped in front of her, his smile engaging. "Please don't tell me I'm the only one who doesn't get a kiss."

Faith hesitated, then grinned as he leaned over so she could kiss the top of his head.

The girls giggled as Faith planted a kiss on his dark hair with an exaggerated smack.

When he straightened, his eyes met hers. "See you later."

Seeing the promise there, Faith smiled. "Count on it."

# CHAPTER NINETEEN

Something was troubling Krista.

Faith saw it the second her friend stepped onto the porch. Still, despite the tired eyes and drawn look, the former model looked breathtakingly beautiful in black tweed pants and a wool-blend sweater that matched the gray skies overhead.

Yet, her friend's normal joie de vivre was missing as she ushered Faith into the kitchen, where coffee perked cheerily in an old-fashioned chrome percolator and freshly baked scones sat on a pretty plate atop the rustic oak table.

The conversation began, as it often did in wintry climates, with talk of the weather.

"I'm glad we didn't get as much snow last night as they forecast." Krista sipped her coffee, the huge diamond on her left hand winking in the light.

"I love snow." Faith smiled at Krista's raised brow. "Though, we've had enough now. Mother Nature can put away the snow-making machine."

Krista laughed, her smile genuine. "I don't know if the skiers and snowboarders would agree."

"Probably not." Chuckling, Faith relaxed against the back of the wooden chair with the pretty cushions. "Oh, before I forget. I wanted to make sure you received the contract I sent last night."

Faith had assumed she'd receive some kind of confirmation from Krista—or from Dustin—but hadn't heard a peep. Not that she'd expected them to agree to the revised terms immediately. She wanted only to know the document hadn't gone astray in cyberspace.

"Yes. Thank you. As far as your request for more time to visit Gatlinburg, take as much as you need." Krista paused. "Dustin and I will pick up the cost of your flight and the hotel stay."

"You don't have to do that," Faith protested.

Krista's gaze met Faith's. "Let me do this. Please."

"Sure. Okay." There was that weird vibe again. "Thank you."

"Ah, how's your morning going so far?" Krista asked, nibbling on a bite of peach scone.

"It's good." Faith smiled, thinking of the scene in the parlor. "Mary was jazzed about the gingerbread house competition. She insisted on handling it herself, though I'd have been happy to help."

Some of the tension in Krista's face eased. "Your grandmother seems like her old self this year."

"It's as if she turned a corner I didn't even realize she was approaching." Faith expelled a happy breath and took a sip of coffee. "Graham and the twins came down right before I left."

If Faith hadn't glanced at Krista as she reached for a scone, she might have missed the shadow that passed over the woman's face.

Could this be what had Krista concerned? Was she worried that Graham wouldn't deliver a campaign they could use and that Faith would be upset if that happened?

"Graham had good news." Faith kept her voice casual as she added a dollop of clotted cream to a piece of scone. "He thinks he's hit a home run with the new campaign. While he didn't show it to me or anything, I think he believes that it's something you'll like."

"Not that it matters," Krista muttered.

Faith lowered her scone back to the plate. Something was definitely going on here. And whatever it was appeared to involve Graham.

"What's going on?" Reaching across the table, Faith grasped Krista's hand. "Please tell me. We're friends."

Krista's fingers closed convulsively around hers. "We are friends. Good friends. That's why this is so difficult."

Maybe it wasn't Graham after all. Could this be about her? Had they decided to pull back on the offer, and Krista had taken on the task of telling her? Was paying for her flight and hotel some kind of consolation gift?

Instead of feeling relief, Faith experienced a twinge of sadness at having the decision taken out of her hands. Sure, she'd gone back and forth, but she still wanted to make the choice rather than have someone lose faith in her. But if it wasn't to be, Faith wasn't about to let this business stuff derail a friendship.

"If you don't want me to take the position, if you and Dustin have reconsidered and no longer think I'm the right fit, I'll understand. This is your livelihood. That's—"

"We haven't reconsidered." Krista's eyes swam with tears. "If there's one thing Dustin and I agree on, it's that you're the right person."

"I don't understand." Faith's head spun. It was as if a mystery had plopped down in front of her with plenty of clues but no solution. "Help me to understand."

"Dustin can get tunnel vision. My husband sees what he wants and goes after it."

"I already know that, or thought I did." Still confused, Faith frowned. "I'm seriously considering the offer, Krista. I wouldn't have had my brother take the time to review the contract if I wasn't. I certainly wouldn't be booking a flight to check out the area."

"Dustin sensed you were wavering." After pushing her plate aside, Krista folded her hands on the table in front of her. "He decided to give a little nudge in the right direction."

"Like paying for my flight and room?"

Krista took in a long breath, then let it out slowly. "What do you know about Graham's previous ad campaign?"

It was like whiplash, Faith thought, this hopping from one subject to the next. Was Krista deliberately trying to keep her off-balance, or were her own thoughts so muddled she couldn't concentrate?

With Krista's eyes on her, Faith answered the question to the best of her ability.

"Graham told me he'd failed to capture the feel of your brand. His error."

"Did he tell you how important it was for him to nail this campaign?"

"Only that he didn't want to lose the account. That he liked your brand and wanted to work with you."

"From what I know, a partnership in the firm is at stake."

"Graham never said anything about that to me." Faith frowned. "How do you know that?"

"Dustin talked to his boss."

A chill, as frigid as a December north wind, crawled up Faith's spine. "Dustin spoke with Graham's boss about him?"

"He did." Krista's tone was matter-of-fact and held no apology. "We had hoped to have the advertising solidified before the holidays. We were both disappointed in the presentation. While it would probably be an excellent campaign for some other product, some other client, it wasn't at all what we were looking for."

"Then why give him another chance?" The small bit of scone Faith had just consumed now sat like a boulder in the pit of her stomach.

"We hoped Graham could pull this off if he went back to the drawing board." Krista shrugged. "We really didn't want to change agencies. We've been working with this advertising group for a while and trust them. Besides, being realistic, we weren't going to find a new firm in a month anyway."

Faith was consumed with the desire to defend Graham. Though Krista hadn't attacked him—they were, after all, merely discussing his work—it felt like an attack. But she kept her thoughts to herself.

This was Graham's career, and the last thing she wanted to do was say something that might make it worse for him.

"I could tell he's excited about this new campaign." Faith nearly cringed when she heard the stiffness in her own voice. She fought to come up with a more equitable tone the same way she fought to hold her coffee cup steady. "I hope you'll like it."

"The content won't matter as long as he delivers what Dustin wants."

The sharp edge underlying Krista's cryptic words snapped the last thread of Faith's control.

"It's obvious you invited me here this morning to tell me something." Faith met Krista's gaze and held. "You've been dancing around it instead of saying what's on your mind. We're friends. That means we can be honest with each other. If there are hard things that need to be said, we say them, straight out. Tell me what has you so tangled up."

Krista expelled a shaky breath. "Last night, Dustin said we needed to talk and that what he had to say concerned you."

Without looking down, Krista crumbled a piece of scone between her fingers. "I was confused, like you are now. What could he possibly tell me about you that I didn't already know?"

Fear slithered like a snake up Faith's spine. "What did Dustin say?"

"He told me he met with Graham Monday night," Krista said finally.

"The night you were in St. Johnsbury visiting your friend."

She nodded. "The night of the storm."

The night, Faith thought, that she and Graham had made love.

"The discussion turned to Gatlinburg and how much Dustin wants you to accept the offer."

When Krista paused, Faith nodded to indicate the woman had her full attention.

"Dustin told Graham he would guarantee that Graham would get our advertising account if he convinced you to accept our offer."

The roaring in Faith's ears made rational thought difficult, but she bore down hard. She had to get answers. No way was she leaving this cabin without answers. "Are you saying Dustin guaranteed Graham would get the account even if he didn't come up with a solid proposal?"

"Apparently—and remember, I wasn't there—Dustin assured Graham we'd work with him until we were satisfied."

"All he had to do was deliver me..." Faith knew she'd spoken aloud, but the words sounded tinny to her ears, as if they came from far away.

"Yes. All he had to do was get you to sign the contract."

Faith's breath came hard. It was as if a vise encircled her chest, making getting air in or out nearly impossible. "Graham agreed?"

Sympathy flooded Krista's face. "According to Dustin."

Sagging back against the chair, Faith closed her eyes and fought for control.

"I'm so sorry, Faith." Krista's voice pitched high, then cracked. "When Dustin told me, I was furious. How dare he treat you, our friend, like some...like some commodity? He denied that's what he was doing and insisted he was looking out for what was best for you."

With great effort, Faith opened her eyes and found herself staring into Krista's concerned ones. She tried to think of some comforting words, but that well had gone bone-dry.

"By the time we finished our…discussion, Dustin understood he was wrong. He offered to meet with you this morning and apologize."

Faith thought of facing both of them and shook her head. "I'm glad it's just you."

"That's what I told him." Krista reached across the table and grasped Faith's hands, knocking her china cup aside. It wobbled in the saucer before settling. "I'm so angry with my husband."

"Graham accepted the offer." Faith voiced the words going around and around in her head. "He agreed to deliver me like a goose on a Christmas platter for thirty pieces of silver."

"I think the contract is worth a little more than that." Krista's teasing tone fell flat.

Despite Krista's attempt at levity, she looked as miserable as Faith felt.

Krista might have released Faith's hands, but concern radiated off her in waves. "Did Graham put on the pressure? Is that why you decided to fly to Tennessee?"

Krista wanted details, but Faith couldn't give them. Right now, she couldn't honestly remember what Graham had said or not said. There was room for only one thought in her head right now.

Graham had sold her out for a partnership.

Had sex been part of the plan? A way to soften her up so she'd be more susceptible to his suggestions? To his subtle pressure?

Her stomach roiled, and Faith was grateful she'd barely touched the scone.

"I loved him." Faith gave a choked laugh. "What a joke."

"I wish this had all never happened." Krista's words tumbled out. "If only Dustin hadn't—"

"I'm glad he did." Dry-eyed, Faith squared her shoulders. "If he hadn't, I'd never have known the kind of man I'd fallen in love with."

~

Graham found himself enjoying the gingerbread house competition. He and the girls stood no chance of winning. That was obvious when he looked around the room and saw all the amazing houses.

"Our house needs a gumdrop right here." With an intense look on her face, Hannah pointed.

"A red one." Charlotte nodded agreement, then glanced at her father. "What do you think, Daddy?"

"I think you and your sister are building something special. Wherever you decide to place that candy will be absolutely the right spot."

Charlotte grinned, lifted the red gumdrop and settled it where her sister pointed.

The jingle that sounded each time the front door opened had Graham glancing up. His welcoming smile came swiftly, but just as quickly disappeared.

Faith stood in the doorway to the parlor, her eyes large and dark in her too-pale face. The knowledge that something was deeply wrong had Graham surging to his feet and telling the girls to finish up without him.

He caught Mary's gaze, and she nodded when he pointed to the girls. They would be in good hands until he figured out what was troubling Faith.

Crossing the room, he held out a hand to her and spoke softly. "What's wrong?"

Faith took a step back and spoke in equally low tones. "Get your coat. Let's take a walk."

Graham didn't hesitate. "I'll be right back."

After sprinting up the stairs, Graham returned moments later with his coat, hat and gloves already on.

He hadn't expected to see Faith back from Krista's so soon.

Had something happened once she got there? Maybe Krista hadn't even been there.

So many questions and no answers.

As they stepped onto the porch, a light snow began to fall. Though the steps and walkway had been scooped earlier and a layer of ice melt applied, he automatically reached for Faith's arm. Not only to steady her, but because he wanted to comfort her, to let her know that no matter what was wrong, he was here for her.

She pushed his hand away.

Puzzled, Graham let it drop. Worry now clouded the high he'd been riding since last night when he'd finally gotten the right feel for the campaign.

His talks with Faith and Ginny had made him realize that a sense of community and family were at the heart of Dustin and Krista's brand.

Once he got that through his thick head, the campaign had come together like a finely tuned watch, each piece fitting perfectly with the other.

Though he was excited to share the presentation specifics with Faith, this wasn't the time. He waited for her to speak, but two blocks went by, and she hadn't uttered a word.

"How did your visit with Krista go?" he asked finally, suffocating under the uncomfortable silence.

"Enlightening."

Graham pondered the response and the bitterness that underscored the single word. He shoved his hands into his coat pockets, hunched his shoulders against the wind. "In what way?"

Faith came to an abrupt stop in the middle of the sidewalk.

The spot where they stood provided no break from the stiff wind. Yet, Graham knew the cold he felt had more to do with the ice in Faith's eyes when her gaze settled on him than the weather.

"Krista told me you and Dustin made a deal." Faith spat the last word as if it was bitter on her tongue.

"Deal?" Even as he asked, Graham knew.

"The one where you sold me out to the highest bidder." Her voice was harsh and filled with raw emotion. "Oh, excuse me. Let me be more specific. The deal in which you bartered my future for a partnership. Sweet deal. For you."

Hurt and anger warred in brown eyes normally filled with warmth and trust.

"I never made any such deal."

Her eyes narrowed. "You met with Dustin Monday night."

"Yes, but—"

"He promised that if you got me to agree to go to Gatlinburg, he would accept your advertising campaign. True or false?" The question snapped in the frigid air.

Graham swallowed against a suddenly dry throat. "He said we'd work on the campaign until we got it right. But again—"

"Dustin made the offer." Her words rolled over him, a steam-roller on a mission.

"Yes." Graham held up his gloved hands. "Full disclosure. He—"

"Full disclosure." Sarcasm dripped from her words. "That would be nice."

With harsh brown eyes pinning him, Graham understood how a trapped animal felt.

"If you'd let me finish, I can explain." He pushed out the words as frustration whipped inside him. How could she judge him without giving him a chance to explain? Graham flashed a tight smile. "When you cut me off like you've been doing, you make me sound guilty as hell."

The fact he felt guilty as hell made it hard for him to defend his actions. But it was important that she know he hadn't sold her out.

"Let me ask you a question." Her gaze settled on his face. "I want you to be completely honest."

"Of course."

"When Dustin made you the offer, what did you say to him?"

Graham expelled a breath. Hope rose. He would explain. She would understand. He had to believe Faith would understand.

"Answer the question."

Her voice was calm now. Too calm?

Graham thought back to the conversation with Dustin. "I don't believe I said much of anything. He did most of the talking."

"When you and Dustin parted ways, did he believe you'd agreed to his offer?"

Graham felt his stomach sink. "I suppose so."

"Because you listened and didn't say anything to the contrary, he assumed you'd agreed." She pressed the point.

"I didn't agree."

"Tacit agreement is still agreement."

"You sound like a lawyer." Graham tried for a teasing tone.

She didn't crack a smile. "If someone made me an offer that, say, offended my sensibilities, I would tell them there was no way I would go along with what they were suggesting. 'Count me out' was one thing you could have said to Dustin. Or you could have laid it on the line and said, 'I won't betray Faith in that way, no matter how much I want that partnership.'"

He sucked in a breath.

"Yes, I know about that, too." She rubbed a mitten across her forehead as if to erase a headache trying to form. "I loved you, Graham. I trusted you. With my heart and with my body. I even dreamed of us figuring out how to build a life together."

She stopped on a choked sob, but almost immediately steadied herself. "I was such a fool."

"You weren't a fool. And I didn't betray you." Graham resisted an almost overpowering urge to pull her to him. "Think back, and you'll realize I never attempted to push you into anything."

"It was always all about you, about what you wanted." With a broad swipe of her gloved hand, she dismissed his plea. "We're done."

Brushing past him, she began walking in the direction of the house.

Struck by the finality in her tone, he called after her, panic edging his voice. "If you love me, don't walk away. We can work through this."

Faith stopped, turned. Her gaze shifted back to him, but for only a second. When she spoke, her voice was as frosty as her eyes. "Don't you see that there's nothing to work through? I won't be with a man I can't trust."

# CHAPTER TWENTY

"I'm sorry to hear this news." Mary's brow furrowed. "I could tell you were upset when you returned from your walk with Graham."

After all the events had concluded, Faith had invited her grandmother into her suite of rooms for cider and conversation. She hadn't seen Graham since he'd helped the girls finish their gingerbread house before heading upstairs.

Though Faith had tried to hide her inner turmoil, apparently she wasn't successful, because she'd caught Mary's worried gaze on her several times during the evening.

Her grandmother had been patient, waiting for Faith to settle and to bring up what was troubling her.

*Troubling her?* Faith nearly laughed at the thought.

Graham's betrayal had flattened her, slammed into her with the force of a Mack truck.

"The worst part is the twins." Faith's heart lurched, recalling how their faces had lit up when they'd seen her. "They were so eager to show me their gingerbread house. I love them, Mary. As if they were my own. It breaks my heart that I won't ever see them again."

"I know you love the girls." Mary sipped her drink. "But it's what is going on with Graham that's breaking your heart."

Closing her eyes against the pain, Faith expelled a ragged breath. "I love him. I wanted to have a relationship with him. How could he have sold me out?"

Which was exactly what he'd done. She remembered the look of guilt on Graham's face even as he'd attempted to defend himself.

"I imagine it's difficult to accept he pushed you to accept an offer that might not be in your best interest." Mary shook her head before picking up her cup.

Faith shifted in her seat. "He didn't exactly push me to accept the offer."

Setting down her cup, Mary studied Faith for a long moment. "I'm confused. You told me about the deal he supposedly made with Dustin."

"There's no 'supposedly' about it," Faith insisted.

The lines of puzzlement on Mary's forehead deepened.

"I think he was trying the subtle approach," Faith explained. "Go in easy, then increase the pressure if I didn't agree."

Mary inclined her head. "Do you really think Graham is that devious? It's certainly hard to reconcile that with the man who's been living here, helping around the house, doting on his two little girls."

"It's difficult for me to accept, too," Faith admitted. "But he told me himself that he let Dustin think he'd agreed and would go along."

"Why did he do that?"

When Faith realized her grandmother was waiting for a response, she shrugged. "No idea."

Mary took another sip of cider. "What did he say when you asked?"

"I didn't go there." Faith waved a dismissive hand. "I'd heard enough."

"Faith."

She'd heard that tone before, and her chin jutted up, just like it had when she was twelve. "The last thing I wanted was to listen to him explain away his behavior."

"You need to talk to him." Steel underscored Mary's words. "You have questions. Now it's time for answers."

"Are you saying I should forgive him?" Faith blustered.

"I'm saying you need all the facts so you can put the matter to bed in your own head." Mary's face softened with sympathy. "Once you have all the information, you can move forward."

Faith raked a shaky hand through her hair. "I'm tired of drama. I just want to go to my shop, do my work and forget all about Graham Westfall."

Mary studied Faith. "Are you still considering Dustin and Krista's proposition?"

"I won't make my decision until after I visit Gatlinburg." Faith gazed down into the cup holding her now lukewarm cider. "I have to see the town, make sure I can see myself living there."

Mary tucked the crocheted afghan more tightly around her. "Who'd have thought your moving here would have led to this opportunity?"

"Do you know what Bryce said?"

If Mary found it odd that Faith's oldest brother had suddenly made an appearance in the conversation, she didn't show it. Mary's eyes went soft the way they always did when anyone spoke of her grandchildren. "What did he say?"

"Bryce sees this as my opportunity to enter the big leagues." Faith's lips quirked upward. "He's decided I'm like him and the rest of the family."

"You are."

Faith's eyebrows shot upward. "I am not."

Mary smiled. "I admit that from the time you could crawl, my darling Faith, you marched to your own beat. You gave the corporate world a try only because it was important to your parents."

Faith thought of the cubicles, the time clock, the routine. "I didn't like it. Or living in the city."

"Yet, you learned a great deal from that experience, so the time wasn't wasted. I believe every experience—good and bad—molds us into the person we're destined to be." Mary's gaze turned pensive. "Your unhappiness in that situation made it easy for you to quit and come to Holly Pointe to care for me."

"I found who I was meant to be here, what I was meant to do." Faith gazed into the crackling fire. "Here, I had the time to take the ideas in my head and bring them to life."

"I'm proud of you, Faith." Mary's words were as soothing as the stroke of her hand. "You've built a business you can be proud of, a business making products that bring joy into the lives of others."

Her grandmother's pride had Faith blinking back sudden tears.

"What I don't think you realize is, if you were truly unlike your family, making a success of your business wouldn't have been such a priority." Even as Mary sipped her cider, her gaze remained on Faith's face. "When you moved here, you had a place to live. You didn't need to soar to survive. But just getting by wasn't enough for you."

Faith inclined her head, the gesture encouraging Mary to continue.

"You're president of the chamber. You're active in other civic organizations. You've built a successful business that's drawn the attention of two hot movers and shakers." Mary tried to suppress a smile, but gave up. "You, my dear, are every bit as driven as the rest of your family. The only differences are you have a more creative bent and are determined to live a balanced life."

Faith opened her mouth, then shut it without speaking. Was

her grandmother's assessment correct? She loved her family. Was being like them really such a bad thing?

"Dustin and Krista have offered you the opportunity to do what you love." Mary leaned forward, and her eyes remained locked on Faith. "Whatever you decide, I know it'll be the right decision for you."

Reaching over, Faith squeezed Mary's hand. "I appreciate your faith in me, in my judgment."

"I'm really looking forward to the Mistletoe Ball on Saturday," her grandmother said, obviously deciding it was time to change the subject.

The planners of the annual event, held the weekend before Christmas, knew how to throw a holiday party. There would be a band and dancing under a rotating mirror ball. Christmas decorations would breathe holiday spirit into the large room.

Romance would be in the air.

Faith's heart gave a tumble. There would be no holiday romance for her this year. No dancing with Graham under the glittery ball as it shot out colored beams of light. No kissing under the mistletoe.

She expelled a sigh. "I've decided not to go."

Mary studied her with thoughtful eyes. "Because of Graham?"

Faith lifted a shoulder, let it drop. "I guess you could say I'm not in a party mood."

After dropping the girls off at Ginny's house, Graham drove up the mountain. Because of a brisk north wind, it was slow going. While the lane had been cleared, the wind kept whipping the snow back onto the road.

Graham nearly turned back. But he needed to clear the air with Dustin before presenting his proposal.

Lights blazed inside the cabin, casting a welcoming glow in

the darkness. Graham glanced at the time. By now, the boys should be in bed. Which meant he'd have Dustin's and Krista's full attention.

Even before he reached the front steps, the door opened.

"Graham." Surprise skittered across Dustin's face. "I didn't expect to see you this evening."

Graham gestured to the door Dustin blocked. "May I come in?"

"Of course." Dustin stepped to the side.

"Who is it?" Krista's voice rang out from inside the cabin.

"It's Graham."

Krista stepped into the foyer, wearing a plush robe over silky pajamas in the same shade of ice blue.

Unlike Faith's nighttime attire, not a single penguin or Christmas tree dotted the fabric.

"Is something wrong?" Krista's gaze shifted from Graham to her husband and back.

"I'm sorry to interrupt your evening. This won't take long." Graham gestured with a hand toward the great room. "Can we sit?"

In seconds, Graham sat in a plush oversize chair that was positioned opposite Krista and Dustin, who sat on a love seat.

Graham placed his bag, holding his laptop and presentation, next to his chair on the floor.

"I'll get straight to the point." Graham focused on Dustin. "As you are obviously aware, Faith knows everything."

Dustin glanced at Krista, then nodded.

"I came here to clear the air. That needs to happen before I present my new proposal."

"Faith said you think you nailed it." Krista spoke to him directly for the first time since he'd arrived.

Graham remembered how excited he'd been. He couldn't wait to show his revised campaign to Faith, couldn't wait to share his life with her…

Now those dreams were in ashes, and Graham had no one to blame but himself.

Bearing down hard against the pain in his heart, he continued. "I should have been upfront from the start. I never intended to pressure Faith. You both need to know that whatever Faith decides it will be her own decision. It will have nothing to do with me."

Dustin rubbed the scruff on his chin. "I shouldn't have put you in that position in the first place."

"I should have never—"

"I think we can all agree that you're both idiots," Krista interrupted. "I hope you've learned from this. Now, Graham, let's see what you've got."

With Christmas less than a week away, Graham and the girls spent most of their time the next couple of days at Ginny's house. Faith worked long hours at the shop, leaving first thing in the morning and not returning home until late in the evening.

"I won't miss this," she murmured, slapping the last shipping label on a package.

She realized with a start that she'd spoken to an empty room. Everyone had already left to get ready for the Mistletoe Ball. She'd stayed behind to finish up.

While she loved this building and everyone she worked with, she realized the majority of her job had become mundane. Billing issues, packaging, supervising employees, everything except the creative.

As the thought rushed over her, Faith realized she'd made her decision. Or, rather, *almost* made her decision.

The trip to Gatlinburg in ten days would solidify it. If she liked the area and the people, Faith would move there, start a new life there.

Without Graham.

The initial hurt and anger had faded. She realized Mary had been right about one thing. She did need answers. Okay, and her grandmother had also been right about the fear. She'd been afraid to tell Graham how she felt. To reach for the dream.

What had Mel told her? *People reach their dreams by going for those dreams. They don't settle. They don't let things happen to them; they make things happen.*

Once the packages were loaded onto the van and on their way for a before-Christmas delivery, Faith drove home with Mel's words echoing in her head.

It was time to speak with Graham. Would he be at the party tonight?

Faith hadn't planned to go. Last night, she'd realized that all she'd done the past couple of days was think. About her business. About Graham. About how difficult it would be to leave Mary and her friends.

This might be the last ball she attended as a member of the Holly Pointe community. Even if she came back next year, she'd be an outsider…

She snorted out a laugh as she entered the house. Sometimes she could be so dramatic. This community would always be home. Her family and friends would always be there for her.

It was Graham's place in her life that was a question mark.

He remained at the forefront of her thoughts as she dressed for the evening. The red velvet gown, its scoop neck edged in satin, dipped low. The sparkly jewels that rested around her neck were family heirlooms given to her by Mary to wear this evening.

The only nod Faith gave to the unique was the ribbon in her hair, subtly imprinted with tiny Santa figures.

Mary was in a jovial mood as she rode with Faith to the party.

"You look absolutely lovely," she told her grandmother for what had to be the zillionth time.

The dress Mary had chosen for the evening's festivities was

long and tailored with lace at the top. The cut and sugarplum color suited her grandmother's slim frame and ivory complexion.

"I feel like my old self." Mary slanted a glance at her granddaughter as she pulled into the already crowded parking lot. "I'm ready to party like it's 1965."

Faith laughed and looped her arm through Mary's as they strolled to the large building. She held tight to her grandmother, not because Mary needed the support, but because they cared about each other, and this evening was about celebrating friends, community and family.

Once they were inside, Mary spotted friends gathered by the punch bowl. She patted Faith's arm. "I'll catch up with you later."

Faith brushed a kiss against her grandmother's cheek, then took a moment to study the room. It was as beautiful as she'd expected. The romantic lighting, the mirror ball over the hardwood dance floor, flowers casting their sweet scent throughout the room. Mistletoe, adorned with red ribbon, hung everywhere.

Mel had been in charge of mistletoe this year and had obviously gone overboard.

"What do you think?"

As if thinking about Mel had conjured her, Faith turned, and there stood Melinda. Her satiny green dress was the perfect foil for her auburn curls.

"I think," Faith returned Mel's hug, "you look amazing. But you went a little crazy on the mistletoe."

"Tell me if you still feel that way by the end of the evening." Mel laughed, a rich, throaty sound. "If you're looking for lover boy, I believe I caught sight of him chatting with Kenny by the appetizers."

Faith hesitated. She'd yet to tell Mel what had happened between her and Graham.

Before she could reply, Mel gave her arm a squeeze. "I gotta go. I'm on a Mom errand. I'll catch you later."

The band had already launched into one of the romantic love

songs that would be a staple of the evening. Elegantly attired dancers and others in their Sunday best crowded the dance floor. Though the music was slow and dreamy now, Faith knew upbeat crowd favorites would be liberally sprinkled into the mix during the course of the evening.

Faith didn't search out Graham. Tonight wasn't the time for them to talk. Not about something so important.

She accepted Derek's offer to dance. For the next hour, Faith flitted from partner to partner.

Once the band took a break, Faith made her way to the refreshment table. Or, rather, she tried to get there. Everyone else seemed to have the same idea.

She changed course, heading instead for a table offering only nonalcoholic beverages. The punch bowl was in sight when she felt a hand on her arm.

"Faith."

For a second, her heart skipped, until she realized the voice was Dustin's, not Graham's.

He held out a hand. "Would you care to dance?"

Faith stared at the outstretched hand for several long beats. Then she smiled.

# CHAPTER TWENTY-ONE

Until the last minute, Graham hadn't been certain he would attend the ball. Things were still rocky between him and Faith. He'd given it a few days—the longest of his life—to settle his thoughts and let her settle hers.

Shawn and Morgan had left with the kids this morning to return to New Hampshire, so they'd done the family Christmas festivities at Ginny's house last night.

The girls had been thrilled with the gifts they'd received and the corny games Ginny had insisted they all play. But on the way home, the girls had asked about Faith and why she hadn't been there, too.

Her absence had been easy enough to explain. This was a family Christmas. Even if he could have invited her as a guest, this was her busy season at work.

He found it sad that the twins accepted the work excuse so readily. If they'd noticed any tension between him and Faith, they hadn't commented on it.

The truth was, he and Faith had been the proverbial two ships passing in the night. He'd seen her coming and going, but never for more than a few seconds.

Tomorrow, he told himself, he would find a time that worked for her, and they would talk.

He almost wished he hadn't finished the campaign, the one he'd previewed for Dustin and Krista, both of whom had given two big thumbs-up. Their enthusiasm hadn't surprised him. The new campaign was as different from the old as he was from the man he'd been when he first arrived in Holly Pointe.

His experiences here had showed him the importance of a balanced life, of melding work with family and fun. That was one of the reasons he'd decided to attend the Mistletoe Ball.

Last night, Ginny had chattered on about how much she was looking forward to having the twins all to herself tonight.

He took a sip of punch and slowly lowered the cup when he spotted Dustin and Faith dancing.

"Hello, Graham."

He turned, and there was Krista, looking like a fairy princess. Except, instead of the pink gown favored by the twins' princess dolls, Krista wore all black with silver accessories.

"It appears they've made up." There was satisfaction in her tone as her gaze remained riveted on her husband and Faith.

"Think if she can forgive him, she can forgive me?"

"Have you asked?"

"I haven't been given a chance." Seeing her with Dustin only emphasized to Graham that he was the big loser in this episode. Worse, he had only himself to blame.

Even if she refused to forgive him, he had to ask. For himself. More, for her.

He couldn't wait any longer. Graham knew Faith's tender sensibilities. He'd hurt as much as angered her. That knowledge brought an ache to his own heart.

Graham set his drink on an empty table and turned to Krista. "Would you care to dance?"

Long lashes swept over cobalt-blue eyes as she gave him a speculative look. "You have a plan."

He only smiled.

She slipped her arm through his. "I have a feeling our dance is going to be the shortest on record."

Faith normally loved romantic ballads, and Dustin was an excellent dancer, but she just wasn't feeling this song. Maybe she wasn't in the party mood.

"Mind if I cut in?"

Pulling her thoughts back to the present, Faith saw Graham and Krista standing beside them.

The green eyes that met hers were solemn. Just like on the day they'd met, Faith couldn't look away. He wore a dark suit, white shirt and… Was that a Bullwinkle Christmas tie?

Faith's lips quirked upward for a second.

"Faith's call," Dustin said smoothly, not releasing her.

"Your husband is an excellent dancer." Faith smiled at Krista. "But I'll give him back."

Krista chuckled, a low, sultry sound. "The man does it all."

Dustin abruptly released Faith and stepped to his wife. "I've got more fancy moves to show you."

Krista trailed a long, glittery silver fingertip down his cheek. "Save the moves for later. Right now, let's dance."

Graham cleared his throat, held out his hands to Faith. "Shall we?"

In a second, Faith was in his arms. It was oh-so-familiar, but instead of relaxing and cuddling close, as she would have only days earlier, she stiffened.

She knew he noticed. How could he not?

"Are you enjoying the party?" he asked.

"I was actually thinking of heading home early."

"I was thinking the same. Great minds and all that."

She found herself smiling and relaxed just a little.

"I want to tell you how sorry I am." He continued quickly before she could say a word. "You were right. I should have let Dustin know immediately I was offended by his offer."

"Why didn't you?" Faith asked bluntly.

"I knew I wouldn't pressure you. You have my word on that, though I don't know why you'd believe anything I have to say." He continued to ramble without taking a breath. "But I wouldn't have. Swear to God. If you look back on all our conversations, I hope you'll see that I didn't."

"I thought maybe you were just going for the ease-into-it-slowly approach."

"Absolutely not."

"Okay." She blew out a breath. "It still doesn't explain why you didn't shut him down."

The green eyes that met hers were filled with clouds.

"Dustin told me if you accepted his offer, they'd tell my boss they wanted to continue to work with me. I figured, what did I have to lose by pretending to go along? I wouldn't push you, but if you did end up deciding—on your own—to take the position, I'd get a free pass." Graham's chuckle held no humor. "The crazy thing was, the thought of having a free pass was enough to free my creative juices. I came up with a campaign they loved in a matter of days."

He paused and searched her eyes.

When she remained silent, pain crossed his face. "You're right. That doesn't negate that it was disrespectful to you. To my character as well. I know it's a lot to ask, but I hope you can find it in your heart to forgive me."

Faith's breath came hard and fast.

It was decision time. When she was growing up, her father had always told Faith that, when she made a mistake, she should take ownership and learn from it. That's what Graham had done.

The only question now was, would she use Graham's stumble as an excuse to not move forward?

Leaning forward, Faith brushed her lips against his. "I forgive you."

Expelling a ragged breath of air, he rested his forehead against hers. "I love you, Faith. Please know I never meant to hurt you."

"We should have talked this out days ago. But I was so hurt and angry—"

"I'm glad we didn't. I needed to figure this out in my head. Come to grips with what I'd foolishly risked for a job."

"Landing this deal means you'll be a partner. You and the girls will head back to the city." Faith swallowed against the lump in her throat. "Unless I'm shocked by what I find, I'll be moving to Gatlinburg."

"I don't want to be hundreds of miles from you."

Faith felt the same. The thought of losing what she'd just found had her wanting to weep. She tightened her hold on Graham and reached for the dream, speaking from the heart. "I don't want to ever let you go."

He searched her eyes. "Then why are we dancing instead of figuring out how to make us work?"

"I don't know if there is a resolution."

"If you want something enough, there is." He kissed her softly as a sweet melody about holding tight to the one you love wrapped around them.

Graham spoke with the girls the next morning. They were enthusiastic about the step he was about to take and eager to take part in the moment. They loved Faith as much as he did.

Last night, he and Faith had discovered much could be accomplished when you put two determined heads together.

As they'd danced, they'd talked. By the time the last melody had faded and the crowd had begun to disperse, the plan had been fully formed.

If he was offered a partnership, he would take it with the proviso that he would work remotely, flying into New York only for meetings that were absolutely necessary. If the promotion didn't come through, or the terms weren't agreed to, he would see it as a sign that it was time for him to branch out on his own.

Graham was driven to succeed. He had ambition. None of that had changed. But he now realized the importance of balance and was determined to embrace that in his personal life.

If Faith didn't like Gatlinburg, she would stay in Holly Pointe, and he would move here. One way or the other, they would begin a life together.

On Christmas morning, he would take the first step toward making their dream of becoming a family a reality.

After speaking with his daughters, Graham made the drive to the Tiffany store in Montreal in under two hours. It didn't take him long to find the ring he knew Faith would love, an Art Deco-style with an emerald-cut yellow diamond in the center. The second he'd seen the vibrant color, it brought to mind Faith—bold and beautiful—and he'd had to have it.

The girls were excited but pinky-swore not to tell Faith. They assured him they liked surprises and wouldn't spoil this one.

On Christmas Eve, he and Ginny accompanied Faith and Mary to church for the candlelight service. Standing beside Faith, the girls next to them in the pew, surrounded by family and friends, felt like a wonderful dream.

Graham nearly asked her that night as they stood in the town square and held hands while singing Christmas carols, the snow falling gently on them.

But he held back. Tomorrow, he told himself, it would happen tomorrow.

~

Ginny was the one who'd come up with the suggestion on how to propose. Until that moment, Graham hadn't realized his mother-in-law had such a romantic nature. They'd involved Mary because she, too, was family.

"You look as nervous as a cat with a new dog in the house," Ginny told him as he pulled into Faith's driveway on Christmas morning.

In the back seat, the girls giggled.

"This is so cool," Charlotte said. "Faith is going to be super surprised."

"What if she says no?" Hannah spoke in a small voice, putting into words Graham's worst fear.

"She won't," Ginny assured her before Graham could respond. "Faith loves your daddy, and she loves you girls."

"Charlotte. Hannah. You know your part?" Now that they'd arrived was a poor time to ask the question, he realized.

"Yep." Charlotte nodded vigorously.

"Move her on to the next spot by giving her another clue," Hannah answered.

"I have bottles of champagne and sparkling cider ready for toasting." Ginny patted her bag, a purse the size of Texas. "I spoke with Mary this morning. She has a lovely celebratory lunch planned."

"But we'll open gifts first." Charlotte glanced at her twin, appearing alarmed.

"Of course," Ginny soothed. "The scavenger hunt first, followed by opening gifts and then lunch. Okay?"

The girls exchanged relieved looks and nodded.

Ginny glanced at Graham. "You have the ring?"

"Right here." Graham patted his pocket and expelled a breath of nervous energy. "I'm ready."

As he said the words, Graham realized he was not only ready for this next step in his life, he was eager. He pushed open his car door and stepped out. “Let the scavenger hunt begin.”

# CHAPTER TWENTY-TWO

Faith originally planned to wear leggings and an oversize sweater, but when her grandmother commented that her red wrap dress was so pretty and festive, Faith chose it instead. While the color was perfect for the holidays, she felt underdressed without a holiday accessory, so at the last minute she pulled a necklace of twinkling lights over her head.

She couldn't wait to see Graham and the girls.

"You've got enough food here to feed an army." Faith shook her head as Mary set the pie she'd just baked to cool on the counter.

"Leftovers are always good to have at this time of year." Mary cocked her head. "Was that the doorbell?"

"I'll get it." Faith stripped off her apron and tossed it onto a chair.

She'd have thought, after all this time, Graham would feel comfortable just walking in. When she jerked open the door, she had to force herself to usher them all inside, help them off with their coats and say a few words to Ginny and the girls before fully focusing on Graham.

Seeing him in dark pants and a gray-striped cotton shirt made her glad she'd dressed up. He looked so positively yummy she could barely keep her hands off him. "I'm glad you could come. Have you had a good morning?"

"I did. Made even better now that I'm with you. Red is definitely your color." Graham took her hands and leaned forward, kissing her gently on the lips. "Merry Christmas, sweetheart."

Faith felt her cheeks warm as the girls giggled.

"Merry Christmas, Ginny." Mary strolled into the foyer, holding out her hands to her friend. "I'm so glad you came."

"I wouldn't miss this for the world."

"Miss what?" Faith asked.

"Christmas, of course. Not to mention Mary's baked ham with the pineapple brown sugar glaze." Ginny gave a little laugh. "And I absolutely adore her mincemeat pie."

Charlotte frowned. "I don't like pie with meat in it."

"Sounds yucky." Hannah wrinkled her nose. "I don't like it either."

"How do you know you don't like it? You've never tried it." Graham paused. "Actually, I don't think I've ever had it."

Mary smiled. "You can all try a bite. If you don't like it, I have pumpkin."

"Can we start the scavenger hunt now? Can we? Can we?" Charlotte begged.

"Please, Daddy, you promised." Hannah folded her hands as if in prayer.

"Scavenger hunt?" Faith glanced at Graham. "What are they talking about?"

"I used to love scavenger hunts around the holidays when I was a child." Ginny cast a pointed glance in Mary's direction.

"I did as well." Faith's grandmother beamed. "There was nothing I enjoyed more than making up clues and sending someone searching for treasure."

"I have clues," Charlotte announced.

Faith turned to the twins and smiled. "Did you make up clues just for today?"

The two nodded in unison, reached into the pockets of their matching red plaid dresses and pulled out scraps of paper.

"We made up a scavenger hunt for you." Charlotte pointed at Faith.

"Me?" Faith brought a hand to her throat. "Why for me?"

Hannah slipped her little hand into Faith's and looked up at her. "Because Daddy likes you, and we like you."

"And it's a fun game," Mary added with a bright smile.

"Totally fun," Ginny added with a decisive nod.

Faith glanced at Graham, the only one who hadn't weighed in on the scavenger hunt.

He only lifted his shoulders and grinned, as if to say, *Don't look at me.*

Charlotte, a future CEO in the making, took charge as everyone stood around looking at each other. She handed one red square of construction paper each to Mary, Ginny and Graham and looked each one in the eye. "This tells you where you should go."

Hannah gave the adults similar-sized pieces of green construction paper. "This is the next clue. The one you'll give to Faith."

Faith glanced from one girl to the other. "I'm impressed."

"We want you to be—"

"Happy," Charlotte cut off her sister. "The game needs to start."

"Shall we take our places?" Mary's eyes glittered as she glanced down at the two scraps of paper in her hand.

It was just one more reason Faith adored her grandmother. Mary was always a good sport and up for any adventure.

Unlike Faith, who'd been hesitant about taking the time on Christmas morning to do a scavenger hunt. Even one especially designed for her.

Which was why, Faith decided, she would go into this one with enthusiasm.

Faith met Charlotte's gaze. "Tell me what I should do first."

"You stand here with me." Charlotte gestured as the others scattered. "In a minute, I'll give you the first clue."

"That works." Faith smiled at the child. "I'm glad you're here."

"You're a nice person." Charlotte studied her. "You're kind and funny, and you don't yell. I don't remember much about my mommy, but if I had a mommy, I'd want her to be you."

Faith noticed she didn't say *just like you*, but that she'd want her to be her. Kneeling down beside the girl, Faith wrapped her arms around her. "If I could have a daughter, I'd want her to be you. I love you, Charlotte."

"Love you back." After giving her a squeeze, Charlotte stepped away, a general once again in control. "Here's your first clue."

*Your bedroom holds one key.*

The first clue took her to her room, where she found Hannah jumping on her bed. With a startled yelp, Hannah hopped to the floor. "Sorry."

"That's okay." Faith sat on the bed, and the girl scrambled up to sit beside her.

Faith wondered if she was supposed to ask for the next clue, or if Hannah would just hand over the paper. "Have you had a good Christmas so far?"

"Um-hum." Hannah nodded.

"Is there anything you want to give me?" Faith paused. Even if the girl had misplaced her paper clue, surely she remembered what it said. "Or tell me?"

"You'd make a good mommy." Hannah flung her arms around Faith's neck. "I love you."

Faith rested her face against this sweet girl's neck. "I love you, too, Hannah Banana."

"I know." Hannah stilled and then pushed at her shoulder. "You have to move on. You can't stay here."

"I don't know where to go." Faith lifted her hands and let them drop. "Do you have the next clue?"

Hannah stuck a hand into her pocket and gasped. "It must have fell out."

She frantically scanned the room until she spotted the green paper on the floor. "There it is."

She dived off the bed, scooped it up, then shoved it into Faith's hand.

*You eat and drink here.*

Thank God for simple clues that even a three-year-old could understand. "I'm off to my next stop."

Before she left, Faith gave Hannah a noisy kiss on the cheek that had the girl giggling.

"You're going to really like the treasure."

"Good to know." Faith found Mary in the kitchen, mashing potatoes. "Am I in the right place?"

Catching sight of the paper in Faith's hand, Mary grinned. "I'd say you're right where you belong."

"Do you have a clue for me?"

"You know, Faith, I've loved every minute of having you in Holly Pointe."

"I've enjoyed every minute of being here."

"I didn't make it easy on you those first couple of years."

"You did the best you could."

"I'm better now. I've got my spirit back, and I feel like I can tackle anything." Mary let out a breath. "What I guess I'm trying to say is, if you move to Tennessee, you'll go with my blessings. Anywhere you go, it will be with my good wishes and love."

"Grandmo—"

"No. Please. Let me finish. Having you here has meant the world to me." Mary continued to mash the potatoes as she spoke. "What will mean even more is seeing you happy and fulfilled—whatever that looks like—in your own life. Understand?"

"I guess." Conscious of Mary's proximity to the stove, Faith gently touched her grandmother's shoulder. "You've never been a burden. If that's what this is about—"

"It's about letting you know that I'm okay. That's all. It's about letting you know that what makes you happy will make me happy."

"Thank you."

"Your clue is under the place mat over there." Mary gestured with her head in the direction of a side table holding a stack of mats.

When Faith peered under the bottom one, she pulled out a red square.

*Go back to the beginning.*

Finally, Faith thought, a clue that wasn't obvious. Yet, she kind of wished it was, well, just a little more obvious. She tapped a finger against her lips.

"To the beginning," she murmured, then started toward the door.

"You're headed in the right direction." Mary lifted the masher and smiled. "In every aspect of your life."

The first thing Faith saw when she stepped into the parlor was Ginny standing near the hearth, a framed picture in one hand.

"Ginny." Faith spoke softly, as the woman appeared deep in thought. "Is everything okay?"

"I brought this over to show Mary." Ginny motioned her close. "These are my kids when they were young."

It was a Christmas picture taken a good twenty years ago. The boys looked like they'd rather be playing with their toys than posing in front of a tree. Then there was Steph, so pretty and full of life, smiling brightly for the camera.

"A lovely family." Faith handed back the picture. "I can't imagine how hard it must be to lose a child."

"Unbelievably hard." Ginny blinked back tears. "That isn't why I brought this photo."

Faith smiled encouragingly.

"None of us knows what the future holds. That's why when we're given a chance to love, to build a family, we need to go for it." Ginny met her gaze. "I hope you know I'd never stand in your way."

Faith suddenly understood. "This is about me and Graham."

"He was a good husband to my daughter, and he's a good father. But he needs more than that. He needs a woman he loves to share his life. To be a mother to my granddaughters." Ginny's smile turned wistful. "I'd love it if I could still be a part of his life after he marries."

Truly perplexed, Faith inclined her head. "Why wouldn't you be?"

"Not every woman is as kind or as generous as you, Faith. That's only one of the reasons I'm glad you're in his life. If things should continue between the two of you, I want you to know that you have my blessing."

Faith sensed these weren't easy words for Ginny to say, but she also knew they came from the heart. Which made them all the more special. "Any woman would be lucky to have you as part of her family."

Without warning, Faith found herself in Ginny's embrace. "Seize the moment, Faith. Don't delay when you know it's right. None of us is guaranteed tomorrow. All we have is today."

Ginny released her, expelling a breath and swiping at tears. "Sorry, I didn't mean to cry."

"I—"

"This is the next clue. I believe, though I can't be certain, it will lead to your treasure." Ginny shoved the paper into Faith's hand. "I need to see what the girls are up to."

Faith's head spun as she read the next clue.

*Up the stairs. You won't need to go far to find your treasure.*

With a resigned sigh, Faith trudged up the steps. The game

had been interesting, but emotionally taxing. She picked up her pace the last few steps and turned the knob of the closed door.

"Here goes nothing," she muttered and shoved the door open.

The first thing she saw was Graham standing beside a huge bouquet of red roses arranged in a crystal vase.

"Are those for me?" She smiled when he nodded. "How did you know I love red roses?"

She stepped to the bouquet, rubbing a soft petal between her fingers. She leaned over and inhaled the sweet scent. "They're absolutely gorgeous. This is a wonderful treasure. Thank you—"

"They remind me of you. You take time to smell the roses, to appreciate the beauty around you." Graham moved to her then, his gaze never leaving her face. "You've taught me that life isn't a race, but a journey. One that we should take time to enjoy along the way."

Faith placed a hand over her heart as it swelled with the sweet words. "Thank you for that."

Smiling, she leaned close and kissed him. "Now, we better make Mary happy and get downstairs. We still need to open gifts before lunch and—"

"She'll wait."

Confused, Faith pulled her brows together. "Wait for what?"

"For me to get out of my own way." Graham took her hand, tugged her to the couch. Even when they both sat, he didn't let go of her hand.

Faith was glad. She liked having her fingers joined with his.

"When I came to Holly Pointe, I wasn't looking for love. In fact, love was the last thing on my mind. I had this big project. I had the girls. In my mind, I had enough on my plate."

She shot him a teasing smile. "Then I swept you off your feet."

"You did."

"I know the exact moment you fell for me."

His lips twitched. "Do you?"

"It was the first time you saw the possum sweatshirt. You

knew any woman who'd wear that shirt was someone you wanted on your team."

He chuckled, then sobered. "I have a team. Two little girls. Not all women want a man with kids."

"If we're talking about *your* girls, I'd say anyone who doesn't want them is crazy." Faith smiled. "Do you know what they told me during this scavenger hunt? They said they love me."

"What did you say to them?"

"That I love them, too, of course."

A softness filled his eyes.

"You know, Faith, during this trip I've learned many lessons, hard ones but ones that I believe will make me a better man, a better father…and a better husband." Graham brought her hand to his mouth and brushed his lips across her knuckles. "I believe to my very core that you and I are a perfect match. I believe we belong together, that we can build a happy life together."

A lump formed in Faith's throat, and she blinked rapidly. "I believe that, too."

"This is for you." He held out a gift beautifully wrapped in shiny turquoise paper with a big white bow.

"The treasure." Faith smiled and lifted a brow. "Is it okay if I unwrap it now?"

His eyes were as dark as jade. "Please."

Faith took her time, carefully sliding off the bow. She removed the paper cautiously, not wanting to rip it.

Though she sensed Graham's watchful gaze, he didn't rush her. With her heart thudding, Faith removed the top of the box, and there, nestled inside, was the angel she'd made as a child.

She glanced up at Graham, and he smiled at the question in her eyes.

"Look at her crown."

Focusing again on the angel, she saw—

"It's a ring." Faith's voice shook as badly as her fingers as she lifted the gorgeous ring with the platinum band and yellow diamond from where it rested against the angel's crown. Her eyes brimmed with tears. "My treasure is a ring."

In one fluid motion, Graham was on his knee before her, taking her hand in his. "*You* are the treasure, my sweet Faith. Your love is the most amazing gift I could ever receive. This angel is part of your Christmas tradition. She's here, with the ring, because I want her to be at the start of a whole lifetime of family Christmas traditions we'll build going forward."

Faith's heart overflowed with love as he leaned forward, gently touched her face, then kissed her softly.

"I could give all kinds of speeches about you being the half that makes me whole," he went on, "or our love being written in the stars, but it wouldn't seem personal enough. What you and I share is unique and wonderful, and there simply are no words to describe it."

"I love you so much," Faith murmured, so focused on him that she barely noticed when he lifted the ring from her fingers.

"I want to spend the rest of my life making you happy. I want you to be my wife and Charlotte and Hannah's mother. I want to build a life with you, have children with you. I promise, if you give me that opportunity, I'll always put you and our family first."

Tears slipped down Faith's cheeks. She didn't try to stop them. They were happy tears, ones filled with joy and the knowledge that every day with this man, every day with Charlotte and Hannah, would be a blessing.

"Will you marry me, Faith?"

It took her only a second to find her voice. "Yes. Oh, yes."

Overcome with emotion, Faith launched herself into his arms. The sudden motion knocked the ring from his fingers, sending it skittering across the floor.

They found it under the sofa, and by the time Graham finally slipped it on her finger, they were both laughing.

"I can already tell our life together is going to be one great adventure." Graham pulled her close. "I can't wait."

His mouth closed over hers before Faith had a chance to tell him that she'd decided a yearly scavenger hunt would make a pretty awesome Christmas tradition.

I'm so happy you got to see Faith and Graham as they found love and their own happy ending. After publishing over sixty-five books I've discovered I love writing books with children. Probably because I have one daughter of my own and three granddaughters. I loved the way this story revolved around family and the wonderful town of Holly Pointe.

If you love heartwarming holiday romance, you're going to want to take a trip back to the first book in the Holly Pointe series, Holly Pointe & Mistletoe. This uplifting romance that brings together Sam and Stella is sure to keep you reading WAY too late at night. Pick up your copy of Holly Pointe & Mistletoe now (or keep reading for a sneak peek).

# SNEAK PEEK OF HOLLY POINTE & MISTLETOE

## Chapter One

Eight days ago Stella Carpenter swore off caffeine. This morning she instructed the barista to add a second shot of espresso to the grande coffee she ordered.

She'd quit because she didn't like being dependent on anything. Or anyone. Excluding, of course, her good friend Tasha, on whose couch she was currently crashing every night.

Shifting impatiently from one foot to the other, Stella pulled out her phone. She had time to wait. Being summoned to your former boss's office demanded a little liquid courage.

The middle-aged man behind the counter held up a cup and cast a glance in her direction. "Stella."

Until she'd been reduced in force from the *Miami Sun Times* three months ago, Stella had visited this particular freestanding kiosk daily. Eduardo had been a barista at this stand since she'd started her job two years earlier.

"It's good to see you again." His voice was as warm as the morning sun. "Are you working out of the office today?"

Her heart lurched as she lifted the cup from his hand. "Just came in for a meeting."

Stella stuffed a bill into the tip jar, then headed in the direction of the beautiful art deco building housing the *Miami Sun Times.*

Even though it was nine a.m. and almost Thanksgiving, heat already rose from the sidewalk, and the hairs on the back of her neck were moist. In southern Florida, there was no hoping for snow on Christmas. When her parents had relocated the family to Miami when she was in her teens, she'd quickly discovered that hot and sunny was the forecast no matter what the time of year.

Stella's heels clicked on the glittering sidewalk as she entered the building that housed the city's largest newspaper. For the past two years, she'd been a reporter and—in a pinch—a photographer and videographer.

Now her job and those of many she'd worked with were gone, replaced by freelancers.

Cool air rushed over her as she crossed the marble floor to the security station. Once cleared, she took the ornate bronze-decorated elevator to the office of Jane Myers, the newspaper's managing editor. The early-morning text from Jane had sent Stella's hopes soaring.

Freelancing had fallen short of paying her bills. It was at times like this that Stella wished her parents hadn't put her inheritance in a trust she couldn't touch until she turned thirty.

She'd been lucky her lease was up. Her first action had been to let her apartment go. The past three months, she'd been bunking on Tasha's couch.

Tasha's roommate had started to grumble about having another person in their small apartment. Last week Tasha had brought down the hammer, telling her she needed to be out by the first of the year. Stella understood, though she wasn't sure where she would go.

Thankfully, she had over a month to figure it out.

When the elevator doors opened onto the fifth floor, Stella stepped out and paused for a long drink of the steaming coffee.

Larissa, Jane's personal assistant, barely gave Stella time to push back her perspiration-dampened hair before ushering her into Jane's office.

Her boss's dark-brown hair was pulled back into a severe chignon. The pale-blue eyes Jane fixed on Stella were firm and direct. The red "cheaters" hanging by an eyeglass chain around her neck added a bit of whimsy, but there was nothing whimsical about Jane's no-nonsense gaze.

"Thank you for coming in on such short notice." Jane rounded the desk. Her stern expression softened infinitesimally.

Stella relaxed when Jane finally smiled but didn't let down her guard. "I was surprised to hear from you."

Jane leaned against her desk as if trying to ease the formal air of the meeting.

"It's been a while since we've talked." Jane inclined her head. "Do you have plans for Christmas?"

Whatever the reason for this unexpected meeting with the newspaper's managing editor, Stella knew it wasn't to discuss holiday plans. She found it odd that Jane was asking about Christmas when they'd yet to get through Thanksgiving. "No plans. I'm hoping to pick up a freelance job or two."

Something flickered in Jane's eyes, an emotion Stella couldn't interpret. Another woman might have launched into a speech about a balanced life. Those words would never make it past Jane's lips. No one was more of a workaholic than her former boss.

Stella inclined her head. "What about you?"

"I plan to have a few friends over. An eclectic group of Miami's movers and shakers. These men and women know where all the bodies are buried. Figuratively speaking, of course. I'm hoping to dig up some juicy kernels."

The comment didn't surprise Stella. Last year Jane had been brought in to shore up the *Sun Times'* bottom line. Immediately after her arrival, the paper began focusing on sensationalized news instead of serious, multisource journalism.

Stella hadn't liked the switch. She would always be grateful she'd been able to work for several newspapers that valued high-quality journalism.

To be fair, the *Miami Sun Times* wasn't the only paper doing what it could to set itself apart. Most were doing all they could to attract readers and increase sales.

"So, Stella. You said you're looking to pick up more freelance jobs before the holidays. Does that mean work has been slow?"

Her assessment caught Stella off guard, as did her expression, which struck Stella as something between concerned sibling and hungry wolf. "Well, no, not exactly—"

"Because I know how hard freelancing can be. Especially with *so many* journalists competing for work."

*Hm,* Stella thought, *wolf it is.*

"I have an assignment for you." Jane straightened, her tone all business. "It will involve travel and approximately six weeks away from Miami. All expenses will be covered."

Before Stella could comment or ask any questions, Jane continued. "If the end product meets with my satisfaction, there may be a staff position available for you starting the first of the year."

Stella kept her expression impassive despite the urge to jump up and do a happy dance. A chance to be back on staff was a dream come true. She'd spent the past three months sending out resumes all over the country but had yet to receive a single bite. "I'm intrigued. Tell me more."

Jane gestured to the guest chair before rounding the large modern desk to sit behind it, formalizing the interaction. Her boss folded her long, elegant fingers and rested them on the shiny onyx.

"Holly Pointe, Vermont, was recently recognized as the Christmas capital of the USA. Not just commercially, the people have been rated as the kindest in the country. The 'capital of Christmas kindness.'" Jane's sarcastic tone told Stella just what she thought of the honor. "I'm interested in doing a feature on the town."

Stella experienced a surge of excitement. This could be fun. Since her parents had passed away, holidays had been especially lonely times. Tasha was spending Christmas with her family in Jacksonville. She'd invited Stella to come along, but she'd gone the previous year and had felt like a fifth wheel. "I love heartwarming features, especially at holiday time."

"I don't believe you understand." Jane leaned forward, her eyes cool and assessing. "I'm not interested in heartwarming fluff. Positivity doesn't sell nearly as well as drama. I want an exposé of the town's underbelly. Whatever dirt there is, I wanted it dug up and in my inbox by December 24."

Stella hesitated. An infinitesimal second, but enough for Jane's eyes to turn to ice.

"I'm trying to help you, Stella, so I offered this to you first. But if this isn't your cup of tea, it's no problem. Juliet is also interested in coming back full time. I'm sure she'd be happy to take this on if you pass."

Though Jane offered no promises, Stella knew that if she delivered, she'd get her job back. Something told her that if she didn't—or if she turned down this assignment—she could also kiss any freelance work good-bye.

"I won't disappoint you." Stella met Jane's steady gaze. "When do I start?"

To read the rest of the story, pick up your copy now! Holly Pointe & Mistletoe

## ALSO BY CINDY KIRK

### *Good Hope Series*

The Good Hope series is a must-read for those who love stories that uplift and bring a smile to your face.

Check out the entire Good Hope series here.

### *Hazel Green Series*

Readers say "Much like the author's series of Good Hope books, the reader learns about a town, its people, places and stories that enrich the overall experience. It's a journey worth taking."

Check out the entire Hazel Green series here

### *Holly Pointe Series*

Readers say "If you are looking for a festive, romantic read this Christmas, these are the books for you."

Check out the entire Holly Pointe series here

### *Jackson Hole Series*

Heartwarming and uplifting stories set in beautiful Jackson Hole, Wyoming.

Check out the entire Jackson Hole series here

Made in the USA
Monee, IL
03 October 2020

43875695R00142